BURIED

MEMORY

A Harbinger P.I. Novel

ADAM J. WRIGHT

ALEC HARBINGER, PRETERNATURAL
INVESTIGATOR SERIES

LOST SOUL
BURIED MEMORY
DARK MAGIC
DEAD GROUND

CHAPTER 1

IT WAS A BRIGHT, HOT summer morning, and as I parked my Land Rover behind the building that housed my office, I felt some of the day's warmth touch my soul. It felt good to be alive. Almost two weeks had passed since I'd moved to Dearmont, Maine, from Chicago, and I felt like I was settling in here. I wouldn't say that the small town felt like home, but I was getting to know my way around and some of the residents even spoke to me on the street. Their conversation was usually limited to a "Good morning" or "How are you today?" but it was more of a verbal exchange than I'd ever had with any of my neighbors in Chicago.

The good folk of Dearmont seemed to accept that a P.I.—Preternatural Investigator— had hung out a shingle on Main Street next to the donut shop.

1

In fact, Felicity had called me from the office this morning to tell me that I had a client. Since the changeling case at the Robinson place two weeks ago, my workload had dried up, making me once again re-evaluate the supernatural potential of Dearmont. I'd come here thinking that it might be a dead zone for cases involving the weird and the strange but the discovery of two changelings and two werewolves had changed my mind.

But since then, there had been no cases to occupy my time. So, I'd been arriving late at the office every morning, which was why I'd been at home beating the hell out of the training dummies in my basement at nine-thirty this morning when Felicity had called to say we had a new client and I needed to come in.

So here I was, freshly-showered and full of anticipation at the thought of a shiny new case.

I walked a short distance along Main Street to the door that had HARBINGER, P.I. printed on its frosted glass panel and went through, ascending the narrow stairs to my office. The smell of warm cinnamon drifted out of Felicity's office, making my stomach growl. I hadn't eaten yet today, and I knew that whatever Felicity had baked, it would taste just as good as it smelled.

I entered her office. "Good morning,"

Felicity was dressed in black slacks, a white top, and black boots. Her dark hair was swept back into a ponytail, and dark-rimmed glasses framed her brown eyes. She was standing by the coffee machine, pouring the contents of the pot into two mugs. Beside the mugs, two cinnamon rolls sat on a small, white plate.

"You sound cheery," she said, adding cream to the coffees.

"Any reason I shouldn't?" I asked.

"No, it's just that I haven't seen you this animated in a while, especially in the morning."

"We have a case," I said. "As long as the client is genuine and not some guy who thinks the face of Jesus appeared in his muffin this morning, I'm happy."

"Oh, this client is genuine," Felicity said, handing me a mug of coffee and the plate of cinnamon rolls. She took a sip of her own coffee and added, "You may have to be careful how you handle this one, though."

I wasn't going to let her dire tone affect my good mood. "Spill," I said. "What's the case? Who's the client?"

She checked the clock on her wall. "She'll be here in about three minutes, so I'll leave that as a surprise."

"Okay," I said, intrigued. "I'll be in my office. Bring her in as soon as she gets here." I took the cinnamon rolls and coffee into my office and placed them on the desk. After sinking into my chair, I bit into one of the rolls. The pastry melted in my mouth and the taste of cinnamon seemed to erupt against my taste buds. Felicity's baking skills were second to none, as far as I was concerned.

I turned on the computer. The usual news sites came up when I opened the browser, including a site that reported local news for Dearmont and the surrounding area. The headlines on that site were usually concerned with bake sales and coffee mornings, although lately, they'd become focused on the murder of local lumber magnate, George Robinson.

George's wife had stuck to the story I'd advised her to tell the police; that she'd found her husband dead and had no idea what had happened to him. The police, having no leads or evidence, hadn't made any arrests. Nor were they likely to, since George's murderer had been a faerie changeling and I'd killed the creature with my sword, along with its partner in crime.

The office door opened and Felicity entered, carrying a tray of drinks and cinnamon rolls and being followed by the last person I had expected to see in my office.

I stood. "Deputy," I said, reaching out to shake the hand of Sheriff Cantrell's redheaded deputy. I knew her name was Amy after hearing Sheriff Cantrell shout it at her, but I would let her tell me how she wanted to be addressed.

"You can call me Amy," she said, shaking my hand with a strong, warm grip. She was stunningly beautiful, with long red hair, high cheekbones, and green eyes. Her uniform did little to hide the curves of her figure.

"Call me Alec," I said. "Please, take a seat." Felicity had been right; this was a surprise.

She sat and spoke a phrase that I'd heard some variant of almost every time a client entered my office: "I'm not really sure why I'm here."

"Hopefully not to arrest me," I said. I'd never used that line before; this was the first time I'd had a cop as a client.

She laughed, but there was little humor in it. I could see that she was going through some sort of inner conflict, probably wondering if coming here had been a mistake.

"Take your time, Amy," I said.

She nodded. "If my dad finds out that I came to you, it's going to cause a lot of trouble." Looking at me intently with her green eyes, she said, "I assume that everything we say in this office remains confidential?"

"Everything regarding your case will be kept confidential between me and my team."

"You have a team?" she asked, looking around at the office. The place was a little bare, with a clock on the wall, a bookshelf full of leather-bound books, and not much else. I really should have made the place a little more welcoming, but I didn't have enough people walking through the door to make decorating a priority. At least the office smelled of cinnamon, which was nice.

"I have a small team," I said. "Miss Lake is my assistant and I have other associates I work with if the need arises. Nobody else will know that I'm working for you, including your dad. Is he against you coming here because of the nature of what we investigate? Many people don't believe that the preternatural world exists."

She frowned at me for a second and then her face relaxed as a look of understanding crossed her features.

"Oh, you don't know, do you? Of course not, you're new in town. My dad is the sheriff."

I almost choked on the coffee I'd been about to swallow. "Sheriff Cantrell?"

Amy nodded.

I tried to wipe the surprised look off my face. Amy looked nothing like her father; he was a big bear of a man with a gruff attitude, where she had delicate features and seemed anything but gruff. She must have inherited her looks from her mother.

"Okay," I said. "So we know why you don't want the sheriff to know you're here; he hates my guts."

"He doesn't hate you. I told you before, he hates what you are, not you, personally. Please don't be offended."

It was kind of hard not to be; being a preternatural investigator was part of who I was, just as being a sheriff was part of who Sheriff Cantrell was. So if someone hated preternatural investigators, I was going to take offense. I didn't tell Amy that, though, because I didn't want to erect any barriers between us. Despite the fact that she was related to Sheriff Cantrell, there was something about her that I liked. I couldn't put my finger on it, but it went beyond her fiery hair and bountiful curves. That sounded crazy even to me; this was only the second time I'd met Amy, so it was way too early for me to say whether I liked her or not. But there it was.

"I can assure you that Sheriff Cantrell won't hear about this meeting from me or my team," I said. "So, what can I do for you?"

"I'd like your opinion on something," she said. "Something strange has been happening at North Cemetery. Last week, Dennis Jackson, the cemetery manger, called us and said that someone had been tampering with the graves. I went to check it out and found some tombstones that had been pushed over and a few mounds in the earth that the manager swore hadn't been there the day before. I told Dennis that it was probably teenagers climbing over the fence at night and making a nuisance of themselves and said I'd get a car to drive past during the nightly patrol. That seemed to placate him, but he called me again two days later, shouting and ranting about grave robbers. I drove over there and what I found shocked me."

She took a folded white envelope from her uniform pocket and slid it across the desk to me. I opened it and removed three photographs, laying them on the desk in front of me. When I saw what was on them, I understood why Amy had come to me for help. This wasn't a simple matter of kids fooling around in the cemetery at night, or even grave robbers.

The photos showed graves that had been disturbed. The earth in front of the tombstones had been churned up and pushed aside, as if the dead residents of the graves had crawled out of their coffins and tunneled up to the surface

7

to escape their final resting place. And sure enough, trails of dirt led from the disturbed graves to bodies lying a few feet away. The bodies were face down and looked as if they had crawled as far as they could before collapsing from exhaustion. But these bodies weren't exhausted; they were dead.

There were two men and a woman. The men wore dark suits; the woman, a dress that had once been bright red but had faded and was covered in clumps of dark earth.

"I know it sounds crazy," Amy said, "but those people crawled out of their graves. The men are Ben White and Ethan Jones. Ben has been dead a little over a year now, and Ethan died last summer. The woman in the red dress is my mother, Mary Cantrell. When we buried her last year, I never thought I'd see her again, but there she was, lying on the grass in the dress she was buried in." Her green eyes filled with tears. I handed her the box of Kleenex I kept in my top drawer.

Keeping my voice gentle, I asked, "What did you do with the bodies?"

She seemed taken aback by the question, as if the answer was obvious and I was a fool for asking it. "We put them back into the ground, of course. Dennis got two of his gravediggers to dig up the graves properly and put the bodies back in their coffins."

"When they brought the coffins up out of the ground, what were they like?" I asked. "Were they damaged?"

Amy nodded, her eyes on the photos. "The lids were smashed, as if those poor people had pounded on them to get out." She looked at me and I could see fear and confusion in her eyes. "I've hardly slept since those graves were filled in. I lie awake at night thinking of my mother and wondering how she … came back to life. Did she think of my dad and me when she was digging her way out of her grave? Was she trying to reach us? She must have felt so lost and alone…." She broke down, unable to stop the flow of tears.

Felicity went over to Amy and put a comforting hand on her shoulder.

Amy soon regained her composure, her professional training probably helping her hide her emotions, push them away until later. "I'm fine," she said to no one in particular as she dabbed at her eyes with a tissue. Felicity went back to her seat.

"You knew this was no ordinary police case," I said. "Did you tell the sheriff about what you found at the graveyard?"

"No, I couldn't submit a report about the dead climbing out of their graves. And I couldn't tell my dad that one of them was his wife; it would devastate him. He took her death very badly last year and the emotional wounds still haven't healed. That's why he hates what you do for a living, because of the way my mom died."

I leaned forward. "Do you want to share that with us? It might be important."

9

Amy nodded and said, "My mom was killed by a preternatural investigator."

CHAPTER 2

$\mathbf{A}$N INVESTIGATOR?" I ASKED. "ARE you sure?" If Mary Cantrell had been killed by a P.I., then she must have been some kind of monster or she was a threat to humans in some way. The rules and regulations followed by P.I.s were clear and had been handed down with barely any change to their wording since the seventeenth century; we were only allowed to kill preternatural beings or humans that were using magic or supernatural forces to harm others.

It was a rule I had technically broken when I'd locked Tunnock in a room with two werewolves, but if I was ever hauled up before the Society and questioned about it, I could claim self-defense, the only other circumstance in which an investigator was allowed to use lethal force.

So why had Amy's mother been killed by a P.I., and did that have anything to do with why she was now crawling out of her grave?

"It was the investigator who worked here before you," Amy said. "Sherry Westlake."

I didn't say anything, but I looked over at Felicity and raised a questioning eyebrow. She gave a slight shrug. Like me, she had obviously thought that I was the first P.I. in Dearmont, that this was the first office the Society of Shadows had opened in the small town. That was evidently not the case.

"Did Sherry Westlake have an office here, in this building?" I asked Amy.

She nodded and looked from me to Felicity and back again with narrowed eyes. "Yes, but you must know that, since you're her replacement."

I nodded noncommittally. "Did she leave town after she ... after your mother died?" I asked.

Amy nodded again. "Sherry Westlake disappeared that night."

I sat back and took a much-needed drink of coffee. I'd thought that the Society had set up an office here in Dearmont to punish me for what happened in Paris, when I'd allowed a *satori* —a powerful mind-controlling creature—to escape the Society's clutches. I'd known that there were corrupt elements in the Society and had decided that the *satori* was too powerful a creature to fall into the wrong hands. When I was kicked out of my Chicago office and sent to Dearmont, I'd had no idea there'd been an investigator here before me.

"Tell us what happened, Amy," I said. "Take your time."

She nodded and took a deep breath. "Before I tell you what happened to my mom, I need you to know that she was a great mother to my brother, Mike, and me. We had a great childhood and she loved us very much. Nothing bad happened until a couple of years ago after Mike moved to New York and I got my own place in town." She sighed. "What I'm trying to say is that all the crazy stuff wouldn't have happened if either my brother or I were still at home. Sometimes, I blame myself for that. If I'd been there for her, she'd still be alive today."

I took another sip of coffee but kept quiet, letting Amy tell the story in her own time.

"Family was everything to my mom," she said after a moment. "She was an orphan and spent a lot of her childhood in foster homes and institutions, so when she met my dad and they had Mike and me, she finally got the family she'd always wanted but never had. She doted on all of us and went out of her way to make sure we were happy. So when we grew up and left home, it left a void in her life. Mike was busy with his job in New York and I was working all kinds of unsociable shifts at the station. I still went to my parents' house for Sunday lunch if I wasn't working, but it wasn't enough for Mom. We'd been her whole life and now we were distant, I guess. She still had

Dad, of course, but he was busy being the sheriff, so she spent a lot of time home alone. All parents go through a period of adjustment when their kids leave home, but it affected her more than most."

Amy picked up her coffee and sipped at it before continuing. I wondered if she would rather be drinking something stronger. It was obvious by the look in her eyes that the story she was telling was one that haunted her.

"Mom finally found something to occupy her time," she said. "She began attending a church over in Clara. That's a small town a few miles east of here. Well, it isn't really a town, just the church and a few houses, really. My mom used to drive over there a couple days a week as well as every Sunday, so the Sunday lunches that had been a family thing became just me and Dad eating together. Mom would eat her lunch with the other members of the church and wouldn't return home until the evening. That's what hurt the most, I guess; where family had been everything to Mom, the church was now her whole life, and became more important to her than Sunday lunch with me and Dad."

"How did your dad react to that?" I asked. From what I'd seen of Sheriff John Cantrell, I was guessing that his reaction wouldn't be too pleasant. He was a man who spoke his mind and had a short fuse. Although, maybe he'd only become like that after the death of his wife.

"He didn't say much about it at first. He knew Mom was having a tough time so he kept quiet. We began having Sunday lunch at my house because Mom's empty chair at the dining table at home was a constant reminder of her absence. Eventually, when Mom began driving over to Clara at night as well as going there in the daytime, Dad confronted her and asked her what was so great about the church that she was never at home anymore. She told him that he wouldn't understand and ignored his pleas to spend some time with her family." She paused to drink more coffee.

"Did you or your dad check out the church?" I asked.

"Of course we did. We pulled the records on the place and ran background checks on the owners. There's been a church in that location for the past two hundred years, owned by a family named Fairweather. It's abandoned now, but the pastor at the time was Simon Fairweather and his record was clean. He lived in Clara all his life and never had so much as a parking ticket. Same with the rest of the family. They've lived in in that small area all their lives. It's like the only reason they exist is to run that damned church."

"Do you think it's a cult?" I asked. "They recruited your mom at a vulnerable time in her life. That's typical cult behavior."

Amy shrugged. "Or it could just be coincidence. All I know is that going there made her turn her back on everything else. I have no idea what the attraction was; I drove over to Clara one day to take a look at the church. The place gave me the creeps."

"So how does Sherry Westlake figure into all of this?" I asked.

"I guess she was investigating the church. She was asking around about it for a while, but nobody in Dearmont knows much about the church, or Clara, for that matter. It's just a tiny township in the middle of the woods, really. I don't know what made her interested in the place. After my mother's death, I tried to find out if someone in town had hired Sherry Westlake to investigate the church but I couldn't find anyone who had, or would admit to it."

I turned to Felicity and said, "We might be able to get our hands on Westlake's files."

Felicity nodded and made a note on her legal pad. If Westlake had disappeared, then the Society of Shadows would have sent a clean-up crew here to gather all her work-related files.

Focusing my attention on Amy again, I said, "So Westlake was investigating the church your mom was a member of, and it all ended badly. Tell me what happened."

"It happened on Christmas Day. There had been a heavy snowfall a few days earlier and my dad was grateful because he thought it meant Mom wouldn't be able to make the drive over to Clara. She'd been talking about going to a Christmas service at the church, even though Mike had flown in from New York and we were going to spend the holiday together, as a family.

"As it turned out, the roads were cleared and Mom drove the Ram over to Clara on Christmas morning. I didn't think about it at the time, but later I remembered that as Mom drove down the street, Sherry Westlake's blue Jeep was following her."

"Do you think Westlake had been waiting for your mom to leave the house?" I asked. "Or could it have been coincidence?"

"The street where my mom and dad live is a dead end, and there was no reason for Sherry Westlake to be there. I probably would have thought it strange at the time if I wasn't so upset about Mom leaving. I was worried about her. Hell, I almost followed her myself." She paused and then added, "Maybe I should have. She might still be alive today."

"What happened next?" I asked as gently as I could. I didn't want her going down the road of regret. I knew that the next part of the story was going to be the most upsetting for Amy and I needed her to stay.

She sighed. "We all spent the day worrying about Mom. We spent most of the morning in the kitchen cooking a Christmas dinner: turkey, potatoes, vegetables, the usual things people eat on Christmas Day. But we hardly ate any of it. Finally, Dad said he was going over to Clara to find out what the hell Mom found so interesting there. Mike and I agreed to go with him. We took my dad's patrol car and drove over to the church."

17

She stopped for a moment. Her eyes looked down at the scarred surface of the desk but I knew she wasn't really looking at it. She was probably unaware of the office, or me, or Felicity. Her mind was replaying whatever image met her as she stepped out of the patrol car at the church.

"It was cold," she said, her voice far away. "There were dark gray snow clouds hanging in the sky over the woods. My dad parked the car in front of the church and got out. There were maybe six or seven other vehicles there, including my dad's Ram, and even though there must have been people in the church, the place was as quiet as the grave.

"My dad rushed up to the door of the church and pulled it open. He's a big, strong man, but what he saw made him fall to his knees and weep. Mike and I ran over to him and we saw what was inside the church. There was blood everywhere, all over the walls and the floors. It covered the windows, turning the cold winter sunlight red as it shone into the room through the blood-stained glass."

Amy looked up into my eyes. "There were thirteen bodies. Men and women. They were lying in various parts of the room as if they'd been flung around like rag dolls. All of them had their throats slit. The coroner said that in all cases, the cause of death was a crushing blow to the body, as if they'd been thrown against the walls or floor with great force. My mom's body was lying near the front of the church. She was face down but I recognized the clothes she'd been wearing when she'd left the house that morning. My dad ran to her and cradled her in his arms while Mike and I stood there in a state of shock. There was a metallic smell of blood in the air so strong that I ran outside and vomited. That brought me out of the shock and I called the state police."

I nodded slowly, trying to picture the scene in my mind. "Was there any other smell in the air inside the church?"

"The smell of death," Amy said.

"Was there anything else? Like the smell of sulfur, maybe?"

"No, nothing like that."

"So why do you think Sherry Westlake killed your mother? There's no reason to believe she would be able to kill thirteen people in that manner."

"The scene was investigated by the state police and the FBI. They found Sherry Westlake's Jeep half a mile away in the woods. They found tire tracks at the church that matched the Jeep. There was blood in the Jeep that matched some of the victims at the church. There were footprints in the snow leading from the Jeep, through the woods to the highway."

"So the evidence is circumstantial," I said. I had no idea if Sherry Westlake had killed those people or not, but there was no way she could have done it the way the coroner suggested. Westlake was a P.I., which meant she was human. The Society had no preternatural creatures on its payroll except for some witches, and they didn't work as investigators. Westlake could have been possessed by a demon, but that was unlikely, since she would have the same magical symbols tattooed on her body as I had, and they protected us from possession by all but the most powerful demonic entities.

"She left that church after everyone else was dead," Amy said. "She didn't call the police or an ambulance. And she hasn't been seen since. If she was innocent, she wouldn't have vanished like that."

"Maybe she was killed," I suggested. "Maybe whatever killed those people chased her into the woods and killed her, too."

She shook her head. "Her tracks in the woods suggested she was walking at a normal pace. Nothing was chasing her. And the tracks led to the highway. She obviously got into another vehicle there and left the scene. The only people killed that day were the thirteen inside the church."

I couldn't argue with her; I didn't have any crime scene photos or case reports to look at. The authorities had constructed a theory about what had happened, which was that Sherry Westlake had killed those people and left the area. The problem was, the people who had constructed that theory were mundane investigators and could only go on what they knew of the world, which didn't include the otherworldly beings that preternatural investigators dealt with all the time. I could think of a dozen creatures that could kill thirteen people in the way the coroner described, but those creatures would never make it into any police report because most people didn't know of their existence.

"I'm sorry for your loss," I told Amy. "Were those two men who crawled out of their graves along with your mother also members of the church in Clara?"

"No, definitely not. Ethan Jones attended Saint Mary's here in town and Ben didn't go to church at all."

"How did they die?"

"Ethan died of cancer and Ben had a heart attack."

"And what happened to the church at Clara after the murders?"

"It closed down. The place is abandoned now, but the Fairweather family still lives there. Simon Fairweather, the pastor, was murdered along with the others, but the rest of the family is still alive."

This was getting us nowhere. There wasn't any obvious connection between the three people that would explain why they'd risen from the grave together. "We'll take the case," I told Amy. "I assume you're not claiming the expense from the sheriff's office."

"No, I'll pay for it myself."

"Do you want me to investigate the church as well? I might be able to find something that isn't in the police records."

She shrugged. "I don't see the point. The police and the FBI have closed the case. As far as they're concerned, Sherry Westlake killed those people. They admit they don't have a motive or know exactly how she carried out the murders, but they're satisfied that she's responsible. She's on their wanted lists."

"And are you satisfied?"

"No amount of investigation will bring my mother back," she said flatly. "Something happened that I can't explain regarding her grave, but I have no illusions; I know she's dead and isn't coming back."

"I'll investigate the church if the investigation of the graves leads there for some reason." I told her.

Amy nodded.

"Felicity will take you to her office to sort out the details and get you to sign our usual contract," I said, looking over at Felicity, who was already getting to her feet.

"Thank you, Alec," Amy said as she stood. "And please be careful to avoid my father. If he knew about what's happening at the cemetery, it would kill him."

"I'll be careful," I said. "At least now I know why he hates preternatural investigators. Luckily, that's a prejudice you don't share."

"Maybe I do," Amy said. "But I have no one else to turn to for help." She left with Felicity and closed the door behind her.

I took a sip of coffee, but it was cold and bitter. So I turned my chair to face the window and looked out over Main Street, bustling with people going about their business, unaware that the dead were rising from their graves in the cemetery. They lived a life I could never live;

a life absent of the knowledge of the dark creatures and forces that inhabited our world. Sometimes, I envied that lack of knowledge, but if I had a choice, I would rather know the truth about the world and be equipped to deal with the nasties rather than be unaware of their existence.

Felicity returned and said, "Everything is sorted with Miss Cantrell. She's paid the usual retainer and signed the contract."

"Great," I said. "Let's take a closer look at those graves. We'll take a crystal shard to detect for magic in the area."

"I'll get one from the safe," she said, turning and heading back to her own office where the office safe was located. I kept some of my minor enchanted items in there for convenience. My most powerful artifacts were stored in my basement at home because the safe wasn't big enough everything, and some of the items had to be stored in certain ways for safety reasons. You couldn't just stuff a safe full of magical objects without consequences, the worst being a possible magical explosion that would rip through the time, space, and dimensional barrier.

There was one item in my possession that wasn't stored either at my office or at home. The gold and silver hieroglyph-inscribed box that I had apparently mailed to myself from Paris was too dangerous to keep close. For one thing, I had no idea what it did, what magical power it had. For another, there were people willing to kill for it and they were connected to the Society in some way. If it was so important to them, it had to hold a great power, a power I couldn't risk falling into the wrong hands. So the box was buried in the woods north of Dearmont. Its location was known only to myself and my friend, Mallory Bronson. Until we researched the box and knew exactly what it was—a task I had set Felicity because research was her area of expertise—it would remain buried.

My cellphone buzzed in my pocket and I pulled it out to answer it. The number displayed on the screen had a 44 code in front of it, which meant the call was coming from Britain. That meant it was probably my father calling from London.

I answered it, and sure enough, it was my father.

"Alec, I need you to come to London," he said, without any further explanation.

"Really, Dad? You think I should just drop everything and fly over there when you didn't even send a team to rescue me when I was stuck in Faerie?"

"You didn't need a team to rescue you. You were fine."

"But you didn't know that, Dad."

He sighed and said his next words slowly, as if he were talking to a five-year-old. "Alec, you need to come to London. I'll send a jet to pick you up. And bring Felicity. I'll let you know when the jet is at Bangor International." He ended the call.

"God damn it!" I shouted, wanting to throw the phone at the wall but resisting the urge. Why didn't he ever listen to me? Or at least pretend he'd been worried about me when I was trapped in Faerie? His timing was lousy; I didn't want to go to London right now because whatever he wanted was obviously Society business, and at the moment, I was none too pleased by the fact that they'd thrown me out of Chicago and sent me here.

Also, the last time I'd been in London was a month ago, when the Society had questioned me about the events in Paris, and that questioning had involved me wearing an enchanted iron collar that the Spanish Inquisition had used to extract confessions from heretics. That had kind of left a sour taste in my mouth where the Society was concerned.

Felicity came back into the office and handed me a small leather pouch containing a crystal shard that could detect magical energy. "Is everything all right, Alec?" she asked when she saw what must have been an expression of frustration and anger on my face.

"My dad called. He wants us to go to London."

"Oh. Did he say what for?"

"Nope."

"So what are we going to do about the graveyard case?"

I stuffed the leather pouch into my pocket. "We're going to take a look at those graves. Come on, let's go."

CHAPTER 3

NORTH CEMETERY WAS, AS THE name suggested, at the north edge of town. Felicity was quiet during the drive over there and I wondered if she was thinking about Jason, her boyfriend in London. He worked for a bank there and wasn't happy that Felicity was over here. A couple of weeks ago, he'd given her an ultimatum: fly back to England to be with him or the relationship was over. As far as I knew, he hadn't made good on that threat yet, and Felicity hadn't gone back there, so they were at a stalemate. If Felicity and I flew to London at my father's request, she would be able to talk to Jason face-to-face and sort out their problems one way or another. I hoped I wasn't going to lose her.

The cemetery was enclosed by a six-foot-high brick wall and had a brick archway that led to the parking lot. As

I climbed out of the Land Rover and saw the beauty of the place, I found it hard to believe that people were trying to get out of their graves here. If I was buried here beneath the manicured grass, shrubs, and trees of North Cemetery, I'd be satisfied with my final resting place. The sun shone brightly on the rows of gravestones, birds sang in the trees, and there was a smell of freshly-cut grass in the air. The parking lot had maybe fifty parking spaces, but only a dozen were occupied. It was a slow day for visiting the dead.

"Wow," Felicity said as she came around the Land Rover from the passenger side. "This place is lovely."

A low brick building with arched windows and a heavy wooden door in a gothic style stood near the parking lot. A sign on the door said OFFICE, so we went over to it and pushed it open. Unlike the exterior of the building, which had been styled to suggest an architecture of days gone by, the office inside was modern and lit brightly by overhead lights.

A young man in a white shirt and black tie sat at a glass and chrome desk, typing on a keyboard, focused on his computer screen. A nameplate on the desk told me the guy's name was Steve McDonnell and he was the Manager's Assistant. "One moment," he said, without looking up. After a few more keystrokes, he turned to us and asked, "How can I help you?"

"We'd like to talk to Dennis Jackson," I said. "Is he here?" I nodded to a door that had Jackson's name on it above a sign that read MANAGER.

"Whether or not he's here isn't really the point," McDonnell said. "The point is whether or not you have an appointment."

I didn't have time for this. I stepped toward his desk but Felicity put a hand in my arm, stopping me.

"I was only going to explain the situation to him," I said to her. To McDonnell, I said, "Tell Mr. Jackson that Alec Harbinger, P.I., is here to talk about his containment problem."

"Containment problem?"

I nodded. "I'd call potentially dangerous dead people crawling out of their graves a containment problem."

"Dangerous?" McDonnell's eyes went wide.

"You've seen zombie movies," I said. "Do you want this cemetery to become a real-life *Night of the Living Dead*?"

"No," he said, getting up from his seat and backing toward Jackson's door. "No, of course not." He knocked on the door, opened it, and disappeared into the manager's office.

Felicity shook her head at me but there was a smile on her face. "That was cruel, Alec."

I shrugged. "Hey, for all I know, there could be a zombie problem brewing here."

"Do you think that's possible?"

28

"I've heard of cases regarding traditional zombies, the ones raised from the dead by voodoo priests, but we won't know anything until we examine the graves."

The door opened and a large black man in a dark blue suit and tie came out to greet us. His expression was friendly, his smile warm. "I'm Dennis Jackson," he said in a manner that was much more welcoming than his assistant's. "Deputy Cantrell said she was going to hire you to look into our … containment problem, as you put it."

"Alec Harbinger," I said, shaking his hand, "and this is my assistant Felicity Lake." While they shook, I asked him, "Can you take us to the graves and show us exactly where you found the corpses?"

"Yes, of course," Jackson said. "We'll take the buggy up there. The graves in question are all the way at the north end of the cemetery." He beckoned us to follow him and went through the heavy wooden door, out into the sunny parking lot.

Outside, he led us around the back of the building to where a six-seater dark green golf buggy was parked. "We use this to take some of our older visitors to the graves of their loved ones."

"That's very considerate of you," I said, climbing into the seat behind Jackson, letting Felicity ride shotgun. I wanted to use the crystal shard as we drove, to check the level of magical energy in the cemetery. The crystal glowed when it detected magic, and the stronger the magic was, the brighter the crystal glowed. I didn't want it to distract Jackson when he should be keeping his eyes on the road.

"We like to take care of our future residents," he said. "Old or young, everyone in Dearmont ends up here eventually." He laughed heartily.

Well, he was a cheery soul. That kind of attitude was probably mandatory in a job that brought you into contact with the bereaved every day. Having a positive outlook was probably the only way to stay sane.

We set off at a speed of maybe ten miles per hour, the buggy's battery making a low hum as we drove smoothly along the asphalt paths that stretched between the rows of gravestones. I took the crystal out of the pouch and held it in my hand. The triangular shard wasn't glowing at all.

While Felicity and Jackson chatted about how hot the day was and how lovely the cemetery looked, I held the crystal at various angles and positions, looking for a telltale blue glow.

Nothing.

Whatever magic had made those three people vacate their graves, it must be more local to where the graves were situated.

"—Isn't that right, Mr. Harbinger?" Jackson asked, finishing a sentence I hadn't heard.

"Sorry? I didn't catch that."

"I was just saying that our jobs are very similar, yours and mine. We deal with areas of life that most people don't want to think about. In my case it's death, and in yours, it's monsters."

"That's true," I said. "The difference is that the monsters fight back. The dead don't … usually."

"No," Jackson said, his tone becoming more serious. "Usually they stay where we bury them." He paused for a few moments and asked, "Do you have any idea what's going on here?"

"Not yet. That's why I want to see those graves."

He nodded and continued driving us north along an avenue flanked with gravestones, mausoleums, and trees. When we finally stopped and he killed the golf buggy's electric engine, we were at the northern boundary wall. Beyond the brick wall, the woods stretched into the distance, gloomy beneath the canopy of branches and leaves despite the brightness of the day.

Jackson got out of the buggy. "This is where we laid Mrs. Cantrell, Mr. White, and Mr. Jones to rest." He indicated three gravestones that stood next to each other but were nowhere near any of the other graves in the cemetery.

"Is this a new section?" I asked. "They're the only three graves here."

Jackson nodded. "The cemetery was built a long time ago, and as you can see, we're butting up against the north wall here. We're filling up fast, so this place here is where we're putting a new line of graves. It'll reach all the way to the east and west along the wall but when we fill all the space, I don't know what we're going to do. Probably have to re-open the old South Cemetery. That place is full and has been for almost a hundred years, but there's plenty of room for expansion into the surrounding land. The government won't let us expand north into those woods beyond the wall, so they're going to have to let us move back to the old South Cemetery or there won't be room for any more graves. We'll be piling the dead on top of each other just because the government wants to save a few trees."

I looked at the three graves huddled together by the wall. The earth in front of the gravestones was dark where it had recently been dug up to re-inter the bodies.

I held up the crystal shard. It glowed blue, but so faintly that it could almost be mistaken for sunlight reflecting off its surface. I moved south, to the graves on the other side of the path. The light in the crystal died completely. I walked north to the graves by the wall. The blue glow intensified. When I reached Mary Cantrell's grave, the blue light emitted by the crystal was unmistakable. It wasn't exactly bright—I'd seen crystal shards glow much brighter—but it was definitely detecting magic in the area. I walked over to Ben White's and Ethan Jones's graves and got the same reading.

"Looks like you got a positive reading in that thing," Jackson said, watching me.

I walked away from the graves, keeping close to the wall. The glow remained the same.

Returning to where Jackson and Felicity stood, I put the crystal shard back into the pouch and into my pocket. I said to Jackson, "I'm sure I can fix this problem for you. It shouldn't happen again."

He raised an eyebrow and looked at me dubiously. "Are you sure? You didn't do anything. Don't you want to see where we found the corpses?"

I shook my head. "There's no need. You can be sure that this won't happen again."

Felicity frowned at me but she remained silent. I'd explain everything to her when we got back to the Land Rover, but not in front of Jackson. "You can take us back to the parking lot now," I said, "and we'll be on our way."

He pointed to the pocket in my jeans where I had put the crystal shard. "Did that crystal fix the problem?"

"Not exactly. The crystal detects magical energy. As you saw, it glowed up here by the wall, but not farther south in the cemetery."

Jackson frowned at me now, his expression matching Felicity's. "Meaning?"

"Meaning the energy is coming from the woods north of the wall. I can deal with that for you. It won't happen again."

"Okay," he said slowly. "If you say so. This is your area of expertise, I guess."

"It is," I replied. "You won't have any more residents trying to escape their graves."

Jackson shrugged his big shoulders. "All right. I'll get my guys to keep an eye on this area, just the same."

"Of course."

We were about to get into the buggy when a voice shouted, "Mr. Harbinger!" I looked along the path to see a wiry man with shoulder-length fair hair running up the path toward us. He wore glasses and had to keep brushing his hair away from the lenses as he ran. When he reached us, he was out of breath, red in the face, and sweating. "I'm glad I caught up with you," he panted.

Now it was my turn to frown. "Do I know you?"

"No, but I know you. Well, I know of you. It's my job to know about everyone in town. Well, not really, my main job is at the store. I own the games store in town. Wesley Jones." He held out a bony hand.

I shook it. His name sounded familiar, but I couldn't place it for a second. Then I remembered; Wesley Jones was the local reporter who wrote articles about coffee mornings, the Dearmont parades, and, more recently, the death of George Robinson.

"I have to ask you," he said, pushing his glasses up the bridge of his nose with his forefinger, "do you know anything about the murder at the Robinson place? I mean, the police are baffled it. Do you think there's a supernatural element to the case that the police are overlooking?"

"No," I said calmly. "I don't. Now if you'll excuse me, I'm on a case right now and...."

"It involves my father, right?" he said. "Ethan Jones, the guy whose grave you've been looking at over there, he's my dad."

"I'm sorry for your loss," I said.

"I knew there was something odd going on when I came to visit his grave this morning," Jones said. "The earth was disturbed and the deputy was just leaving. Is it vandalism, Mr. Harbinger? Witchcraft? Satanism? Those are the things you deal with, right? Well, probably not vandalism."

"Not vandalism," I said. "That's a police matter. Mr. Jones, I really have to go."

"Call me Wesley."

"Wesley, I have to go. It was nice meeting you." I climbed into the back of the golf buggy. Jackson and Felicity got in and we set off down the path, the electric motor humming softly. I looked back at Wesley. He was standing at his father's grave, staring down at the recently-dug earth there. I could have told him that there was nothing out of the ordinary happening here but he was probably too smart to believe that. I was just thankful he'd arrived this morning when Amy had been leaving. Any earlier, and he might have found his father lying in the cold morning sunlight.

Jackson dropped us off by the Land Rover and thanked us for coming. He still seemed unconvinced that the problem would be solved but he had no other choice than to accept my word for it.

When we were in the Land Rover, Felicity asked, "Why did you tell him it won't happen again?"

"Because it won't. You saw the crystal; it was detecting energy in the woods north of the wall. There's nothing special about those three graves; they just happen to be the only graves close enough to the north wall to be affected by the magical energy in that location."

"Okay, I understand that, but where is the magical energy coming from?"

I pointed to the north end of the cemetery. "Those woods north of town are where I buried that box."

"The hieroglyph box?" Since we didn't know the actual name of the gold and silver box, we called it "the hieroglyph box" for the sake of convenience.

I nodded. "It's leaking magic and the leaked energy is raising those people from their graves. That's why I told Jackson it won't happen again. All we have to do is move the box farther north so the energy doesn't reach the graves."

Felicity nodded, her brows furrowing as she became lost in thought. "This will make my research much easier. I should be able to find the box in the Society's database now I know what its purpose is."

"Yeah," I said, starting the Land Rover's engine. "Its purpose is clear; the box raises the dead."

CHAPTER 4

AN HOUR LATER, WE WERE walking through the woods toward the spot where I'd buried the hieroglyph box. The woods were shady and cool as Felicity and I trudged through the undergrowth, but the relative comfort of the air temperature was offset by swarms of tiny insects that buzzed around us. They were annoying enough for me to swipe at them with the shovel in my hands but all that did was disperse them for a few seconds before they came back with a vengeance, biting my neck and face. They didn't seem to bother Felicity much. She flicked her hand at them a couple of times but otherwise didn't seem bothered by the tiny terrors.

The place where the box was buried was unmarked. I didn't want a random hiker investigating the area and finding the box. So instead of leaving a physical mark on the ground, I'd recorded the exact longitude and latitude of the box's location on my phone.

"It's here," I told Felicity, when my phone's GPS told me we were at the right spot. I put the phone in my pocket and began to dig.

Felicity sat on a fallen branch and watched me. She'd been quiet during the short walk from the road but now that I saw her face, I could tell she wanted to say something but was trying to find the best way to say it.

"What's up?" I asked her.

"I was just thinking about London," she said. "Do I really have to go with you?"

"What, you don't like my company anymore?" I dumped a shovelful of dirt onto the ground.

"It isn't that, Alec. It's just that if I go back there, I'm going to have to face Jason."

"You've been avoiding him, huh?" I thrust the blade of the shovel into the soft earth.

She nodded slowly. "Yes, I suppose I have. He wants me to choose between going back to England and being with him, or staying here and us splitting up. I love it here and I love my job, but I thought Jason was the man I was going to spend the rest of my life with, so it isn't an easy decision. I thought that by avoiding the issue, I'd be able to put off making that decision, but if I go back to London, I'd have to see him face-to-face and give him an answer."

"You really should come with me," I said. "I don't know why my father wants me to go to headquarters but it must be something important, and I'd like you to be there." I grinned, trying to lighten the mood. "I've gotten used to you. And you make great coffee."

She shot me an exasperated look. "Oh well, at least I'm good for something, even if it is only making the drinks."

"You're good for a lot of things," I said, digging deeper into the earth beneath the tree. "I'd like you to come to England with me because I value your input."

"Oh," she said, taken aback. "Thank you, Alec."

"And I may need cinnamon rolls or apple bakes while I'm there, and you're the best baker I know." I shoveled deeper, inwardly cursing myself. I couldn't just compliment Felicity and leave it at that, could I? I always had offset the compliment with a joke and ruin it.

The tip of the shovel contacted the heavy cloth I had wrapped the hieroglyph box in before I'd buried it. I bent down and scraped the remaining dirt away with my hands, lifting the cloth-covered box out of the hole. I unwrapped it and looked at its shiny gold and silver surface etched with perfect, tiny hieroglyphs. If it had just been a decorative piece, it could be the centerpiece of any ancient Egyptian museum exhibit.

But it wasn't decorative; it was dangerous. The box contained such a powerful magical energy that it had caused three corpses to climb out of their graves. And that was just a tiny fraction of its power. Who knew what would happen if the box were activated in the proper manner?

I had to bury this thing far away from here, in a place where it couldn't cause any more trouble. These woods were huge, covering miles of territory to the north before reaching another town, so there were plenty of places to hide the box where it would be isolated, its power unable to affect anyone.

Felicity leaned in close to my shoulder and stared at the box. "I know it might be an evil artifact that could destroy the world," she said, "but it's beautiful."

"Destroy the world?" I asked her. "Where did you get that idea?"

"It has to be important, Alec, otherwise why would you have mailed it to yourself from Paris and why would someone be trying to kill you for it? In fact, you said they were trying to kill you simply so you couldn't use the box's power against them. Doesn't that alone mean it must be super powerful?"

"Yeah, I guess so. But as for mailing it to myself, I can't remember why I did it. Hell, I can't even remember doing it at all." I turned the box in my hand, sunlight reflecting off its surfaces. "If only we could decipher these hieroglyphs."

"I'm still working on it," she said, looking into my eyes. "There's a set of the photos of the box next to my computer in the office and another set next to my computer at home. The symbols on the surfaces are in some sort of code and without a key, I can't break the code."

I was aware of Felicity's closeness, the heat of her body, the fragrance of her perfume. I wondered if my desire to take her to London with me was more than just professional. Maybe I wanted her to have to confront Jason so she would split up with him. With him out of the way....

I pushed the thought from my mind. The poor girl was distraught about the ultimatum her boyfriend had given her and here I was seeing it as an opportunity for myself. I needed to get a grip and focus on the task at hand.

Rewrapping the box, I said, "Let's find a better resting place for this thing."

We began the hike back to the road where I'd left the Land Rover. When we emerged from the woods and onto the road, I was surprised to see Amy Cantrell's police cruiser parked behind my Land Rover. When she saw us coming out of the trees, Amy got out of her car and waved us over.

"Dennis Jackson called me and said you'd fixed the problem," she said. "Is that right?"

"Yeah, it won't happen again," I told her.

She nodded, looking as unsure about my claim as Jackson had. "So what was it that made those people come back to life?"

"There was a magical item buried in the woods near the north wall of the cemetery. It was leaking energy and that energy animated the corpses." I looked into her green eyes and said, "They didn't come back to life exactly. The magic just made them move. What you said at the office about your mother being lost and confused, that isn't true. She wasn't actually brought back to life."

"Okay," Amy said. "Well, that's a comfort, I suppose. So what are you going to do with the magical item? Is that it, there?" She nodded at the cloth-wrapped box in my hand.

"Yeah, this is it. I'm going to put it somewhere where it won't cause any more trouble."

"Can I see it?"

I didn't see any harm in letting her see the box, so I unwrapped it and held it up to show her.

"Wow, that's pretty. You say it's magical; what does it do?"

"It raises the dead."

She looked at me like I was being a wise ass. "No kidding," she said sarcastically.

"We didn't know that until now," I said. "We've been doing research and trying to determine what it is. Now we have more to go on."

Amy nodded slowly, looking into the trees as if she were thinking about something. Then she turned her attention back to me and said, "This magic stuff, it's real, isn't it? I mean, you believe in it."

"I know it's real," I said simply.

She stood with her hands on her hips and turned slightly to look south toward where the cemetery was situated, even though the trees shielded it from her view. "I'd like you to do something for me," she said quietly. Then she turned to face me and said, "I want to hire you to investigate that church in Clara."

"All right," I said. "I can do that."

"Good." She sighed. "I thought I was certain about how my mother and those other people died but now I'm not so sure. Maybe there are more things in this world than I or the FBI agents investigating the case know about, and maybe something has been overlooked."

"I can look into it for you," I said, "as soon as I get back from London."

"London?"

"Yeah, I have to go there on business." I didn't mention the Society. Most people assumed that P.I.s were self-employed, working for themselves. It didn't occur to them that we were organized by a secret society formed in the seventeenth century to combat the supernatural forces in the world. Without the use of the Society of Shadows' resources, most P.I.s would be floundering in the dark.

The Society provided us with enchanted weapons, artifacts that were useful in the hunting of supernatural forces, and, maybe most importantly, a huge online database of creatures, rituals, potion recipes, spells, and magical items that had been compiled from just about every magical grimoire and lore book known to mankind through the ages. We also had some of the actual books, bound in leather, with pages that smelled of mildew and age. They were pretty cool.

"Okay," Amy said. "That's fine. It isn't like it's going to change anything anyway. Those people will still be dead and Sherry Westlake is in the wind. Your investigation will be a matter of closure more than anything. I want to make sure no stone has been left unturned."

"If there's anything to find, I'll find it," I said.

"Thank you. And I don't need to remind you that...."

"Your father won't know anything about it," I assured her.

She smiled, but I could tell she was wondering if she was crazy or not for hiring me. After months of believing that her mother had been killed by a P.I., I'm sure I was the last person she'd ever considered hiring. But that was before her mother had crawled out of her grave.

Which reminded me—we needed to get the hieroglyph box to a safe burial site.

"I'll be in touch," I told Amy.

"Sure." She got back in her cruiser and drove back toward town.

I turned to Felicity and held up the box. "Let's get this thing back in the earth. We'll head north for a few miles and then hike back into the woods before we bury it." We got into the Land Rover. "And then we can take a look at that church," I said.

"I thought we were going to do that when we got back from London."

"Sure, we'll start the investigation then, but we can take a look now. Just to get a feel for the place."

Felicity shrugged. "Okay, that suits me. I was going to spend the rest of the day doing research anyway. Now that I know what the box does, it should be much easier to find on the database. In fact," she said, reaching into the back of the Land Rover to grab the laptop I kept under the seat there, "I can get started on that now." She balanced the computer on her lap and opened it up.

A half-hour later, I pulled over on a deserted stretch of road and checked a map of the area. We were in the middle of nowhere, an ideal place to bury the box.

"I've got it!" Felicity said. She'd been typing on the laptop all the way here, entering various searches into the Society's magical items database. She turned the laptop so I could see the screen. There was a black and white drawing that was unmistakably a representation of the box on the back seat.

The title above the drawing looked ominous.

"The Box of Midnight," I said to Felicity. "Oh great. Sounds harmless."

"That's a loose translation from the ancient Egyptian," Felicity said.

"Okay, so what does it do?"

She spun the laptop so she could see the screen and typed a couple of keystrokes to bring up the description of the Box of Midnight. Her face went pale as she read.

Looking at me, she said, "It was used by an evil sorcerer in ancient Egypt to raise an army. An army of the dead."

CHAPTER 5

THREE HOURS LATER, WE WERE eating cheeseburgers in Darla's Diner. The mouth-watering smell of fried meat and onions that drifted from the kitchen at Darla's was one of my favorite things about Dearmont. And the burgers tasted every bit as good as they smelled.

I'd buried the Box of Midnight as far away from civilization as I could and I'd made sure the hole was deep. Just its name gave me the creeps, so I wanted to make sure it was in an isolated location where nobody was going to find it and buried deep enough that its energy leak wouldn't affect anything.

After all the digging and hiking through the woods, my burger tasted even better than usual. Darla's burgers were always amazing, but having just hidden a powerful, dark magic artifact made me feel like I'd earned this piece of Heaven in a bun.

"What I don't understand," I said to Felicity a through a mouthful of meat and cheese, "is why someone thought I could use the box against them. What's that about? If it raises the dead, I don't see how I'm going to use it against anyone. It isn't like I'm going to raise an army of zombies to defeat my enemies."

Felicity had the laptop on the chair next to her. She opened it and put it on the table, eating her burger absent-mindedly, her brown eyes wide behind her glasses as she became absorbed in her work, trawling the Society's database.

I watched her, thinking that of all the P.I.s in the entire Society of Shadows, I must be the one with the cutest assistant. Hell, most investigators didn't even have assistants. The only reason I had one was because my father had sent Felicity here to spy on me. I had no idea what he hoped to gain from that.

"It might be something to do with this," she said, spinning the laptop around to face me. The screen showed a drawing in the same style as the one of the Box of Midnight, only the item in this picture looked like a staff inscribed with hieroglyphs instead of a box. Its name was apparently the Staff of Midnight.

"The Box of Midnight and the Staff of Midnight," I mused. "I'm guessing the two items are related."

She consulted the computer and nodded. "They were made to work together. The box contains magical power, like a battery, and the staff directs that power. Whoever holds the staff controls the power in the box."

I shrugged and took another bite of my burger. "I still don't get it. I only have the box, I don't have the staff, and it sounds as if the box is useless without the staff and vice-versa."

She ate in silence for a moment, tapping away at the keys and concentrating on the screen. After a couple of minutes of reading, during which time I finished my burger and started on my fries, Felicity looked at me over the thick rims of her glasses. "What if the person who wants to kill you has the staff? According to what it says here, the staff has no power of its own; it has to be in the vicinity of the box before it can do anything. Once it's close enough to the box, the wielder of the staff has the power to raise the dead and make them do his will. The box itself holds the power but doesn't actually do anything. Like I said before, it's just a magical battery."

"But that," I said, pointing a French fry at her, "doesn't explain why the person who sent Tunnock to kill me told Tunnock that as long as I was dead, the location of the box was irrelevant. If Tunnock's employer has the Staff of Midnight, he needs that box to work it. So telling Tunnock it doesn't matter where the box is doesn't make sense."

"Actually, it does," Felicity said. "Remember, Tunnock saying that if he killed you, you couldn't use the box against his employer? But the box can't be used in any way, so that's what doesn't make sense. Until you realize that the box and the staff are linked. You can use the box against the person who holds the staff."

"How?" I asked.

"By destroying it. If you destroy the box, the staff is useless."

"Makes sense," I said. "But what if Tunnock had killed me? His employer would never know how to find the box that powers the staff."

"He would know eventually. The Staff of Midnight and the Box of Midnight are inextricably linked to each other by powerful magic. The staff will eventually lead its wielder to the box."

I thought about that for a moment. "Does that work the other way around too? Could the box lead us to the staff?"

She shrugged. "Yes, I think so."

"So maybe that's why this person doesn't want me to live. Maybe he thinks I'll use the box to track him down and kill him."

"Or her," Felicity added.

I nodded. "Or her."

"That's a reasonable assumption. It sounds like something you would do."

I wasn't sure if that was a compliment or insult. I chose to believe it was the former. "It does," I said. "If this person has the Staff of Midnight, then they obviously want to use it to raise an army of the dead. I can't allow that to happen."

"I know," Felicity said. "That's why I said that tracking them down is something you would do." A light smile played over her lips.

So, it had been a compliment after all. I returned her smile and then said, "We need to find out how to use the box to find the owner of the staff. We also need to know how to destroy it, just in case we don't have any other option. At least destroying it will ruin the plans of whoever has the staff."

She nodded and went back to typing. She began reading the text on her screen again. Then she wrinkled her nose and said, "Ewww."

"What is it?" I asked, leaning forward over the table to see what she was reading.

"I just found out what's inside the box. There was a sorceress in ancient Egypt during the 18th Dynasty, named Tia, who cast spells and enchantments for the pharaoh, Amenhotep. According to legend, the high priest of Heliopolis, a man named Rekhmire, was jealous of Tia's power and found a way to harness it for himself."

Felicity paraphrased the words she was reading on her screen. "He cut out her heart one night and magically sealed it inside a gold and silver box inscribed with hieroglyphs. He murdered her at midnight on the night of the royal jubilee, so the box became known as the Box of Midnight. Rekhmire created the Staff of Midnight and used it to raise an army of the dead to march against the pharaoh. But his plan failed, his undead army was destroyed, and Rekhmire disappeared, along with the box and the staff. The box and staff have appeared on the underground antiquities market over the years but their whereabouts is currently unknown."

"Well, we know where the box is," I said in a low tone. Darla's was a busy place and the hum of conversation from the tables and booths, as well as the clatter of cutlery and other sounds that came from the diners around us, meant that we probably couldn't be overheard by our fellow customers. But I was still cautious. For all I knew, my enemy could be sitting at the table behind me, listening in on my conversation with Felicity. Hell, they didn't even need to be sitting in the diner; there were plenty of magical ways they could eavesdrop on us, too.

As a precaution, I took the crystal shard from my pocket and removed it from its pouch. Placing it on the table, I watched it closely for a telltale glow.

Nothing. The shard remained dull. At least we weren't being spied on. I put the crystal back into its pouch.

"Destroying the box isn't so easy." Felicity said, watching me stuff the pouch back into my pocket. "The box is magically locked and only opens when the staff is being used to direct its power. At that time, the box opens, exposing Tia's heart. It says here that if the heart is stabbed with a blade, it will die."

"That sounds easy enough," I said. "We wait for the bad guy to show up with the staff and when the box opens, we stab the heart." I dipped my last French fry in ketchup and popped it into my mouth. "Then I kill the bad guy."

Felicity shook her head. "It isn't that simple, Alec. There's a curse built into the box. Whoever destroys the heart of the sorceress will have only one year to live from that day."

I sighed. "Why couldn't ancient sorcerers keep things simple? Those guys cursed everything in sight. Okay, new plan: we wait for the bad guy to show up and kill him before he can use the staff."

"Or she," Felicity added.

"Or she."

"This bad guy, as you put it, will have considerable power of their own. If they're even attempting to use the Staff of Midnight to raise an army of the dead, they must have some serious magical knowledge and experience."

I shrugged. "And I have some serious enchanted swords."

She closed the laptop. "I'll do some more research later and see if I can find out anything else about the box."

My phone buzzed. I looked at the new text on the screen and frowned. "Crap. My dad is sending a jet to pick us up tomorrow. We need to be at Bangor International in the morning."

Felicity's face fell slightly. I guessed that she'd been so absorbed in her work that she'd forgotten about Jason and London. Now, instead of thinking about long lost civilizations and ancient curses—which Felicity loved— she had to turn her thoughts to more mundane matters. The disappointment was obvious in the way her face softened and her eyes dropped from mine to the surface of the table between us. She let out a slight sigh and nodded slowly. "Okay. I'll need to go home and pack."

"Yeah," I said, "the church will have to wait. Hey," I reached across the table and touched her hand for a brief moment. "We'll be back here before you know it."

Her eyes remained fixed on the table. "If I ever come back at all."

CHAPTER 6

I DROPPED FELICITY AT HER house and she got out of the Land Rover, muttering, "See you in the morning, Alec," before closing the door and walking down the driveway to her front door. We had driven there in silence, Felicity sitting sullenly in the passenger seat, staring through her window but probably not seeing what was out there.

Her statement at the diner that she might not be coming back had shocked me. As far as I was concerned, Jason sounded like a dick. The fact that he had given Felicity an ultimatum proved it. Her decision to leave him should be easy.

At least, that's what I thought. I didn't know all the facts, but from what I did know, I had thought that there was no way Felicity would even be considering moving

55

back to England permanently. Now that I knew she was considering it as an option, I felt like someone had punched me in the gut.

I drove to my house, which was just next door, and parked next to Mallory's orange Jeep Renegade. The Jeep, which had been battered by werewolves a couple of weeks ago, had just come back from being repaired and looked as good as new. Because Mallory had been assisting me on a case at the time, I'd claimed the vehicle repairs as an expense related to the case and the Society had footed the bill.

Running my hand over the smooth bodywork of the Jeep, I had to admit that the repair work was undetectable.

"Looking good, huh?" Mallory came out of the house and joined me in the driveway. She was wearing jeans, army boots, and a tight black T-shirt. Her long auburn hair blew slightly in the warm breeze.

"Looks amazing," I said.

She patted the Jeep. "Now that she's all fixed, I can get out of your hair for a while. Maybe I'll go visit my sister for a while before I resume my hunt."

"No leads yet?" I asked as we went into the house.

She shook her head. "No crazy killings involving occult symbols carved on the victims' bodies anywhere. Unless there's a police force somewhere keeping it quiet." She looked at me with concern in her hazel eyes. "It isn't like Mister Scary to go this long without leaving a bloody mess somewhere. I'm afraid I might lose the trail completely. What if he just disappears?"

"He won't," I said. "You'll get a new lead." I went into the kitchen and poured us both coffee from the pot. As I handed Mallory the mug, I said, "But if you don't have anywhere to go right now, I'd like to ask you a small favor."

She arched an eyebrow. "Why do I get the feeling this favor is anything but small? I'm not putting my Jeep in danger again."

"No, this really is a small favor. All I want you to do is hang around for a couple more days while I'm in London."

"That's it, huh? I just stay here until you get back?"

"And make sure nobody gets their hands on the box. I sent the coordinates of its new hiding place to your phone."

"Yeah, I saw that. Anyone in particular I should be wary of?"

"Well, if anyone arrives in town with a staff that can raise the dead, you need to be particularly wary of them."

"I'm pretty sure that would get my Spidey sense tingling," she said.

I told her about the Staff and Box of Midnight, the fact that the box contained the heart of an ancient sorceress known as Tia, and the legend of the curse attached to destroying the heart.

When I'd told her everything that Felicity had found on the computer, Mallory grinned. "You've really got yourself involved in some deep shit this time, Alec. Armies of the dead? Ancient curses? Sounds dangerous."

"So will you guard the box while I'm gone?"

"Hell yeah, count me in."

"Thanks, Mallory. Contact me the instant anything out of the ordinary happens, okay?"

"Of course. So, are you taking your lovely assistant Felicity to London with you?"

"Yeah, my dad wants her to go to headquarters with me. He probably wants to question her about me. He sent her to spy on me, after all, so he's interested in me in some way, even if he doesn't usually show it."

"He's interested, Alec. You're his son."

"He didn't even send a rescue team when I was stuck in Faerie."

"You weren't stuck in Faerie."

"He didn't know that. Felicity called him and told him I'd been gone for five days. That should have been enough for him to be concerned. He should have sent that rescue team."

"He didn't have to," Mallory said, looking into my eyes, "because he knew you'd be okay. He has total trust in you."

I wasn't so sure about that. I drank the last of my coffee and put the empty mug in the sink. "If he trusted me, he wouldn't have sent Felicity to spy on me."

She frowned. "Hmm, you have a point."

"Want to go down in the basement and train?" I asked her.

She looked at me with a mock-sultry look. "How can I refuse an offer like that?" she asked huskily.

I laughed. "Come on, we can spar with the swords. Have you been practicing?"

"Enough to beat your ass," she said as we descended the steps to the basement. The entire basement area was dedicated to training. With a heavy bag, an assortment of training dummies, free weights, kettlebells, a rack of weapons, and a large padded area for sparring, it had everything I needed to stay fit and sharp. The only drawback to having a training area in the basement was the lack of ventilation, which meant the place smelled faintly of sweat all the time. I'd placed large fans in all corners of the room to keep the air circulating but the basement still smelled like a gym locker room.

I'd learned to use various weapons at the Academy of Shadows and most of those weapons had been archaic, like the sword and dagger. These were deemed by the Society to be the best way to kill monsters and every investigator had to be highly proficient in their use.

When I'd first met Mallory, she'd been conducting her own personal manhunt for Mister Scary, the killer responsible for an event dubbed by the media as the Bloody Summer Night Massacre. Mallory, using only her wits, improvised weapons, and a great deal of courage, had survived that event. In fact, she had been the only survivor, dubbed the Final Girl by TV stations, papers, radio stations, and news sites all over the world.

I had taught her everything I knew about fighting with edged weapons, as well as some blunt ones such as fighting sticks and *shinai*, the cane weapons used in Kendo. Mallory had been focused and diligent in her training and despite me asking her earlier if she had been practicing, I knew she spent as much time as she could with the weapons or just beating hell out of the training dummies and heavy bags. She was driven by a desire to find and kill Mister Scary and that drive motivated her to train hard.

We removed our footwear and stepped onto the mats that covered the floor in the sparring area. Mallory grabbed two *bokken*, wooden training swords shaped like *katana*, and tossed one over to me. I adjusted my weight so I was balanced on the balls of my feet and gripped the *bokken* lightly in both hands. Mallory did the same, facing me with a determined look in her eyes.

I attempted a swift, sneaky blow before we had even agreed to start, arcing my sword at Mallory's midriff. She was ready for it. Stepping back slightly, she countered my strike with an expert block. The wooden blades made a loud *thunk* when they connected. The sound echoed around the basement.

"Good," I said, stepping forward, resetting my position. "You were ready for that attack."

"I was ready for you to cheat, if that's what you mean," she said, feinting to the right. I fell for it and lifted my sword to block the blow I thought was coming from that direction. Mallory reversed her movement and landed a blow on my left thigh. The impact of the solid wood against my muscle made me wince. These may have been training swords but they could still deliver a painful blow. My natural reaction was to step back but I forced myself to ignore that instinct and stepped forward, thrusting the tip of my sword at Mallory's shoulder. It connected, spinning her around, throwing her off balance.

I moved forward to follow up the strike by sweeping my wooden blade against Mallory's legs. She was already stumbling so I aimed to make her lose her balance completely and send her sprawling to the mat, but I hoped that she had remembered the counter move I'd taught her a while ago against such an attack.

I felt a sense of satisfaction when she thrust her sword down to block my attack and then planted her feet firmly on the mat, regaining her balance. I was so busy being pleased that I failed to notice the wooden blade of her sword swing up toward me. By the time I saw the move, I felt the impact of Mallory's *bokken* against my ribs.

Mallory stepped backward, out of my reach, and grinned. "Trying to get me on the ground? You'll have to do better than that, Alec."

"Okay," I said, "I'll stop holding back."

She laughed. "Oh, of course, you're holding back. Why didn't I notice that? Could it be because … you aren't?"

She lunged forward suddenly, swinging her sword at my shoulder.

I crouched and brought up my own sword to block the blow. The blade *thunked* together for a brief moment and then parted as Mallory began a second attack, this one aimed at my arm.

I threw myself back onto the mat, rolling out of the way of Mallory's attack and springing to my feet as she jumped forward to attack me a third time. Mallory's sword described a perfect arc as she struck at chest height. I parried the attack, the blades whacking together noisily. If that attack had connected, it would have hurt.

Mallory was sweating and panting, a determined expression fixed on her pretty face. She was giving it her all, desperate to land a strike.

I was totally on the defensive, trying to avoid being hit by her attacks as they rained down on me. I deflected two more strikes, then a third that had been aimed at my head. I moved out of Mallory's reach, giving myself time to catch my breath. "Hey, that last one was a little too close for comfort."

"Maybe you should stop holding back then," she said, grinning.

"Oh, so you want to play rough, do you?"

She braced herself, sensing that I was about to attack.

But I didn't move forward with my sword in hand. Instead, I threw the swords at her face, knowing she would bat it away with her own sword but hoping that would give me time to shoot under her defenses and take her down to the mat.

My sword spun through the air toward Mallory and I followed it, staying low, planning to grab her around the waist and overbalance her.

Mallory batted away my sword as I'd known she would but she also side-stepped out of my way. My momentum sent me sprawling to the mat, knocking the air out of my lungs. I rolled onto my back, ready to get up, but Mallory was on top of me, straddling my chest, trying to pin my hands with her own. Her sword was gone, tossed to the mat next to mine.

She looked down at me, breathing hard, her chest rising and falling rapidly beneath her T-shirt. Her long hair brushed my face. It smelled of peaches.

I was too strong to be pinned by Mallory but I had to admit I was enjoying being in this position, so I didn't struggle too much.

"I win," Mallory said, looking down at me, her pretty face framed by her tumbling auburn hair.

"Okay, okay, you win," I said. Then I added, "Unless I planned for this to happen,"

"No way, Alec, you didn't plan any of this."

I grinned. "Still, I end up being straddled by a beautiful girl, so who's the real winner here?"

Her expression softened slightly and she dropped her face to mine. Our lips met and we kissed long and hard.

My hands slid out from beneath Mallory's and went to her waist. I held her there gently while we kissed.

After a couple of beats, she pulled away and got to her feet. "Alec, I'm sorry, I shouldn't have done that."

I sat up on the mat. "Hey, don't blame yourself. It was my fault just as much as yours."

"I'm sorry," she repeated, pacing back and forth on the mat. She was anxious, on edge. Her hands balled into fists then released over and over while she moved like a caged animal.

"Mallory, don't get upset over this," I said. "We'll just forget it ever happened."

"Like the last time we kissed? And what about the next time? How many times will be trying to forget things that happen between us?"

"I'm only saying to forget it because...."

"I know why you're saying it, Alec. When I asked you to help me get over my fear of sex, I told you it was a no-strings-attached arrangement. And that worked out just fine ... for a while. But now, it's becoming confusing. It's becoming more than what it was supposed to be."

I went to her and put my hands lightly on her shoulders. "Is that a bad thing? Who says we can't just see where this leads?"

"I say." She pulled away from me and stalked over to the area where the heavy bag hung from the ceiling. "I'm broken, Alec. Mister Scary ruined my life. He ruined me."

She lashed out at the bag with a right hook, followed by a left.

I wanted to go to her, to hold her and tell her that everything would be okay, but I had the feeling that would only make things worse. I let her take out her frustration on the heavy bag. Eventually, her punches weakened and she sank to the ground.

That's when I went to her. I sat on the floor next to her and put an arm around her shoulder. She leaned against me and whispered, "Will I ever be okay, Alec?"

"You're okay now," I told her.

"Just okay?" she asked, a trace of humor returning to her voice.

"Well, I don't want you to get too big-headed," I said.

She looked at me and said, "Thanks, Alec," before kissing me lightly on the cheek and getting to her feet. "I need to hit the shower." As if all her concerns were suddenly forgotten, she hummed to herself as she walked to the shower room.

"I need to go pack," I told her. "You want pizza tonight?"

"Sounds good to me," she said before she closed the door to the shower room. A few seconds later, I heard the shower start up. Then Mallory began singing.

I went upstairs, feeling bad for her. She was trying her best to stay positive but I knew that the lack of leads regarding Mister Scary's whereabouts was getting her down. I also knew that Mallory's mental defense against feeling low was to tell herself that once Mister Scary was dead, her problems would vanish. I was pretty sure that wouldn't happen, but I wasn't going to shatter the only illusion that gave her hope of working past her issues.

Hell, for all I knew, maybe killing Mister Scary *would* cure her of her problems. I wasn't a therapist, just a concerned friend who would be there to offer support if Mallory needed it.

In my bedroom, I chose the smallest piece of luggage I owned—a weekend bag—and placed it on the bed. I didn't intend to spend much time in London; I needed to be back here as soon as possible to deal with whoever was after the Box of Midnight. Whatever my father wanted could probably be dealt with by email or a phone call but he had a penchant for face-to-face meetings, even if it meant I had to fly halfway across the world to be told some scrap of information that he deemed too important to trust to electronic communication.

I'd just finished throwing a few items of clothing into the bag, reminding myself that it would be colder in London than it was here, when the doorbell rang.

"I've got it," Mallory shouted from downstairs.

Then, a minute later, she shouted, "Alec, Felicity's here."

Deciding I'd packed more than enough for a brief trip to London, I closed the weekend bag and put it outside the bedroom door on my way downstairs. I found Felicity in the living room, along with Mallory, who was dressed in gray sweats and drying her hair with a towel.

"Alec," Felicity said, "I've found something I think you'll be interested in." She looked much happier than she had when I'd dropped her outside her house. In fact, she seemed to be excited about something. She had a folded piece of paper in her hand but I couldn't make out what was printed on it.

"Okay, what is it?" I asked.

"You may want to sit down," she said, indicating the sofa.

I sat, wondering what could get Felicity so excited. Mallory was perched on the arm of the easy chair and had stopped drying her hair for a moment, obviously as intrigued as I was by Felicity's manner.

"I think I know how to get your memory back," Felicity said. Her dark eyes flickered from me to Mallory and back again.

"How?" I asked.

"First I need to explain something. As well as researching the Box of Midnight, I've been looking into magical ways of restoring lost memories. Since you told me about Paris and the fact that you can't remember what happened there, I thought it would be important for you to get those memories back. Especially because it was during that time that you sent the Box of Midnight to yourself."

"Okay, so what did you find?"

"There was a statue in ancient Egypt of a god named Hapi. He was supposedly responsible for the flooding of the Nile every year, the flood that irrigates and nourishes the barren land. Well, it seems that in the city of Heracleion, on the banks of the Nile, there was an eighteen-foot-tall statue of Hapi that was said to have magical powers. Just as the god supposedly brought the flood to restore the land, so could the statue restore things to the mind of anyone who touched it and recited a magical formula. As you know, most Egyptian magic is based on sounds and words. I did a study into the theory of magical sonics a couple of years ago when I…."

"The statue, Felicity," I said, bringing her back on track.

"Yes, of course, the statue. Where was I? Oh, yes, the statue had the power to restore things to the mind. People went to the temple and, under the guidance of the priests, touched the statue and recited the formula to remember things they'd forgotten. Some people did it to remember dreams. So I was thinking the statue could help you remember what happened in Paris. Maybe its power could unlock that magical door in your head."

It sounded reasonable. I didn't have any better ideas for getting my memories back. "Where was this statue?"

"In the temple at Heracleion."

I cast my mind back to the lessons on ancient Egypt I'd taken at the Academy of Shadows. "Didn't the city of Heracleion sink into the Nile?"

"Yes, it did," Felicity said, nodding. "In the year 800 A.D."

"So we're going to have some trouble finding this ancient statue."

"No, we're not," she said, unfolding the piece of paper she'd been holding. "Look at this." She held it in front of my face so I could see what was printed on it.

It was a flyer for the British Museum in London. Felicity had printed it from the museum's website. There was a photo of a diver swimming next to the head of a large statue on what looked like a riverbed. The flyer was advertising a special exhibition at the museum called Sunken Cities and promised that the treasures of the sunken cities Heracleion and Canopus were on display from May to November

"Is that the statue?" I asked Felicity, pointing to the statue in the photo.

"Yes, that's the statue. And it's on display right now at the British Museum in London."

"So you'd researched the statue and tonight you found out that it was at the museum in London, where we're going tomorrow?" It all sounded too coincidental. I became paranoid when pieces fit together so neatly, because that synchronicity might mean that magic was involved somehow.

Felicity shook her head. "No, I was looking at what shows and exhibitions were on in London at the moment and I found this on the British Museum's website. You know how much I love relics and antiquities. I'd come across the statue of Hapi in my research already but I didn't put two and two together until I saw it on the website."

"I see." So she'd been looking for places to visit in London during our trip. Probably somewhere to take Jason. I wondered if he shared Felicity's love of relics and antiquities.

"So is it worth a try?" she asked me. "I can find the magical formula from the old Egyptian texts that are scanned on the database."

"Won't the statue be behind glass or something?" Mallory asked.

"Probably not," I said. "They keep some items behind glass there but most items, especially larger ones, just have a 'Do Not Touch' sign next to them." I turned my attention to Felicity. "Okay, if you can get that formula tonight, I'll give it a shot. There's nothing to lose, except being kicked out of the museum."

"I'll go and find it right away," Felicity said, heading for the door.

"We're ordering pizza," I told her. "You want to bring your laptop over and do the research here?"

Her dark eyes flickered to Mallory then back to me. "No, thanks. I've got a microwave meal waiting for me next door."

"Okay, but if you change your mind, just come over when you see the pizza guy."

She smiled, but it seemed forced. "Thanks, Alec. I'll see you in the morning." She left and I locked the front door after her.

When I returned to the living room, Mallory was shaking her head slowly at me.

"What?" I asked.

"There's no way she was going to stay for pizza, Alec. You know she doesn't like me."

"What do you mean? Of course she does."

Mallory pointed her finger at me than back at herself. "She's confused about what's going on here."

"Between us?"

She nodded. "Look at it from her point of view. You've known me for years. We've been living together for the past two weeks. She sees how easy we are in each other's company. It makes her feel uncomfortable. She's confused."

"No, she isn't."

"Alec, even *I'm* confused about us."

I shrugged. "I don't see why the situation between you and me would make Felicity feel uncomfortable."

She raised an eyebrow. "Really? You're going to play dumb?"

"Felicity has a boyfriend."

"You mean the boyfriend who is going to dump her if she stays here? The boyfriend who works at a bank? Hmmm, let me see, a boring accountant who works at a bank or a preternatural investigator who hunts and kills

71

monsters? Nah, there's nothing to choose between you two."

"Very funny. I'm going to order the pizza. What do you want?"

"Pepperoni. And don't act dumb with me, okay? I know you like Felicity. I'm not going to turn into a banshee and trash the place just because you find her attractive."

"If you turned into a banshee, I'd have to kill you," I said.

"Don't try to change the subject."

"I like her," I said, "but I work with her. She's a good assistant and I don't want to do anything that would affect our working relationship. And you may joke that there's nothing to choose between me and Jason, but if that were the case, why is she so torn about her decision to stay here or move back to England and be with him?"

"Is she? That's surprising. I thought she'd stay here for sure."

"Me too," I said, "but we must be underestimating her relationship with Jason. And England is her home, so she could be homesick, too."

"Wow, so you might be coming back here without her." Mallory looked as surprised as I was at that possibility. Felicity had only been around for a little while, but she'd fit right in and become a part of the "gang" that had helped in solving the Robinson changeling case.

"Yeah, it's possible," I said, shrugging in an attempt to cast off the heaviness that settled in my gut whenever I imagined Felicity leaving. "Hey, it's not like I'm even supposed to have an assistant anyway. She's only here because my dad sent her. I've worked alone before; I'll just have to do it again."

Mallory was silent for a moment, then she said, "I hope she comes back with you."

"Me too," I said. Then I added, "But that's only because she's a good assistant and I'd like to help her put in the required time in the field to become a fully-fledged investigator. I don't have any romantic inclinations toward her." Even as I said that, I wondered if I was kidding myself, but I had to forget about any kind of romance with Felicity. She was far away from home, she had a boyfriend, and I had feelings for Mallory. It was complicated.

"Okay," Mallory said, in a voice that told me she didn't believe a word of what I'd just said. "But if any of that denial is to do with your feelings toward me, you might as well forget about them now. I'm broken. And until I kill the bastard who broke me, I'm too screwed up to enter into any kind of relationship."

"If it's because we can't have sex, I don't mind about...."

"I mind," she said. "I can't go on living in fear. And until I destroy that fear, I'm not going to enter into a relationship where there will always be an issue like that, a huge-ass elephant in the room. I just need to take out

Mister Scary, erase him from the face of the planet, and everything will be okay again. And I can't ask you to wait until then."

"I'm willing to wait," I said.

"I know you are, and that scares me a little. We're in too deep, Alec. Neither of us is really facing that fact, but that doesn't make it any less real."

"I know it doesn't," I said. "I'm just saying that if you wanted me to wait until you get Mister Scary, I would. If you want me to help you find him, I will."

She shook her head, her wet hair brushing her neck. "That's something I have to do. Anyway, Mister Scary isn't a preternatural being, so he's not really your problem."

"He is my problem. He's hurt you. Anyway, he might be preternatural, for all we know. Or using magic to carry out the murders. The occult symbols he carves into his victims' bodies kind of points to that."

"I need to take him on my own, Alec," she said simply.

"Okay," I said. I respected her decision to go after Mister Scary alone, but I didn't like it. The guy was a serial killer, and if he was using magic as well, that made for a lethal combination that might be out of Mallory's ability to handle.

"You know what I'm looking forward to the most?" she asked, her voice light again.

"Seeing Mister Scary dead at your feet?"

"Yeah, but I was thinking more along the lines of a pepperoni pizza."

"Right," I said, getting my phone out of my pocket and scrolling through the contacts list. I had all the local fast food joints listed in there, as well all my favorites from Chicago. I should probably get around to deleting the Chicago ones at some point. It didn't look like I was ever going back there.

Forty minutes later, the pizza guy arrived and delivered Mallory's pepperoni and my meat feast. We watched *Jessica Jones* on Netflix while we ate and I told Mallory that her dress sense was like Jessica's. Combat boots, jeans, T-shirts, and leather jackets.

"I don't mind that," she told me through a mouthful of pepperoni pizza. "Jessica's cool."

I nodded, "She is."

"And she faces her problems head on."

"She does." I wanted to add that even if Jessica managed to get the bad guy at the end of Season One it wouldn't make her life perfect. Her problems would continue into Season Two.

But I said nothing.

CHAPTER 7

THE NEXT MORNING WAS COLD and gray as Felicity and I were ushered by two black-suited men in shades across the tarmac at Bangor International Airport and onto the Society of Shadows's private jet. The men looked identical in build and had identical stoic expressions. If it wasn't for the fact that one of them was bald and the other had long shaggy hair, I'd guess that they were clones of each other. The plane was unmarked, of course. It didn't have "Society of Shadows Airlines" painted on the tail with a symbol of a pentagram or anything. It was nondescript and unremarkable, much like the guards in their secret service attire.

Felicity was dressed in her white blouse and black pencil skirt, making me the odd one out in my casual attire.

Jeans, boots, a T-shirt, and my favorite flannel shirt were the perfect clothes for a flight as far as I was concerned.

As we boarded, Felicity asked one of the shade-wearing men how long it would be before we arrived in London. He ignored her question and showed her to her seat.

"They won't speak to you," I told her as I took the seat across the aisle from hers and fastened my seatbelt. "I've tried to strike up a conversation before; there's no point."

"Oh, I suppose I'll have to speak to you, then."

I laughed. "Nice to know I'm your last choice for someone to chat to."

She looked flustered. "No, I didn't mean it like that, Alec. I'm sorry."

"Don't worry about it. I could tell by the way you were quiet all the way here that you have more on your mind than idle chit-chat." She'd spent most of the drive from Dearmont looking out through the windshield at the dark road ahead or drifting in and out of a light sleep. I'd remained awake, of course, which was a good thing since I was driving, fueled by two strong coffees and a promise to myself that I'd sleep on the plane. At the moment, that was all I wanted to do: close my eyes and catch up on the sleep I'd missed getting up early to drive to the airport.

"It's a long flight," I told Felicity. "There'll be plenty of time to chat." I folded my arms, adjusted the position of my seat, and closed my eyes. I really wasn't a morning person, so it would be better for everyone concerned if I got a few hours of shut-eye now and tried to be sociable later.

I was asleep before we took off.

When I awoke, we were thirty thousand feet over the Atlantic. I checked the time on my phone. I'd been asleep for six hours. Felicity was sitting in her seat, listening to something through white earbud headphones. I roused myself with a few stretches. My back ached. I hated flying.

Felicity picked up her phone from the seat beside her and turned off whatever she'd been listening to. Removing the headphones, she looked across the aisle at me. "Have a good sleep?"

"No, I don't sleep well on planes."

"You seemed to be doing a good job of it."

"What are you listening to?" I asked her.

"A lecture on ancient and magical languages."

"Sounds riveting."

"It's very interesting, actually. It was recorded at the Academy of Shadows a few years ago."

"Maybe I was there, then. If you hear snoring coming from the audience, that's probably me."

She shot me a disapproving look. "You act like you don't care about any of this stuff, but you've acquired the knowledge somehow. You don't just pick up all that knowledge without having a passion for the subject."

"You do when you've been living at the Academy since the age of ten."

"What? Ten? Really?"

"Yeah, after my mom died, my dad made sure I was going to follow in his footsteps, so he sent me to the Academy of Shadows as a residential student. Most of the other students there were much older than me so I had to learn how to protect myself from bullies. I was always more interested in the combat classes than the language lectures, but I guess the language stuff rubbed off on me after a couple of years."

"I'm sorry about your mother," Felicity said softly.

I shrugged. "It was a long time ago. She died in a car accident."

"Oh, that's terrible. Were you in the car too?"

"No, I was at my aunt's house. We lived in Oregon at the time, in the town where my mom was born. She took me there after she left my dad because that's where her family lived. She said she wanted me to have a normal childhood and not spend it learning about the preternatural world. So, I had a few years of living just like any other kid. I had friends, I went to school, and I had a loving family around me. When my mom was killed, my dad arrived in Oregon and took me to London, to study at the Academy of Shadows."

Felicity said, "That sounds terrible. To be taken away from your family like that and sent to a boarding school at the age of ten. I can't imagine what that would be like."

"I grew up fast," I said. "I had to. I was determined that I wasn't going to be the little kid everyone pushed around, so I learned to fight. And yes, I did studying the ancient languages, but that wasn't because I had a passion for it; I just wanted to be better than everyone else. I enjoyed learning about preternatural creatures and lore, but I think I've forgotten most of those language lessons. That's why it's useful having you around. You love that stuff."

She smiled. "Yes, I do. My father and mother were both Egyptologists and they passed their love of ancient things on to me. Although they'd be shocked if they knew that the dusty old relics they were studying had real magical power. Or that the hieroglyphs could be used in real spells." She laughed lightly.

"Are they still alive?" I asked.

"Yes, they live in Sussex."

"And what do they think you do for a living?"

"They know I work for a preternatural investigator in America, but they think that preternatural investigators are charlatans fleecing gullible people of their money."

I smiled at that. "Well, maybe that's not a bad thing to believe. It must be comforting, in a way."

"Yes, I suppose so." She paused for a long time and then said, "They want me to marry Jason. It's their dream to have their daughter married to a wealthy banker, with a nice house and a couple of kids. You know, the usual thing."

"Yeah," I said. "I think that's the kind of life my mom wanted me to have. So, Jason's wealthy, huh?"

She groaned and sat back in her seat, looking up at the ceiling of the airplane. "There's more to life than money. That's what I keep telling my parents, and now it looks like I've got to tell you, too. Jason's financial position means nothing to me."

"I get it," I said. "I keep telling myself that there's more to life than money, especially when I don't have any."

She sat forward again, leaning across the aisle, her dark eyes suddenly excited. "But don't you see how great your life is, even though you're not rich? You fight monsters, you keep people safe from the things that inhabit the darkness. You're like a knight in shining armor. I couldn't imagine you doing a mundane job like banking."

"No, I guess not."

"What do you think your father wants to speak to you about? Do you think it's a case of some sort?"

"I have no idea. The truth is, this trip couldn't come at a worse moment. I need to be in Dearmont in case some nut-job turns up and goes after the box. I don't like leaving Mallory there alone."

Felicity nodded. "You care for her a lot, don't you?"

"Yes," I said. "I do."

"If I … stayed in England, do you think Mallory would work with you? The way I am now?"

"No, that wouldn't happen. Mallory will leave eventually to hunt down Mister Scary. It's what she does."

"So you wouldn't get a new assistant to help with cases and running the office?"

"No, it isn't usual for investigators to have assistants. So I'd be working cases on my own and the office would become a mess, much like my Chicago office was."

She grinned, not sure if I was joking or not. I wasn't. My Chicago office had been as untidy as any private eye office you'd see in an old movie. It wasn't that I liked mess, or had a romantic image that I was Sam Spade or someone like that; I just didn't have time to clean.

"Was Chicago your first posting as a P.I.?" Felicity asked.

"No, I wouldn't be trusted in a big city like that, even though I only worked the East side. My first assignment was in a small town in Ontario, Canada, near Algonquin Park. I worked closely with another P.I., a First Nations guy. He was a good investigator and we worked some interesting cases. Werewolves, wendigos, and faeries, mainly."

"Then Chicago?"

"Then Chicago. I really liked it there and I thought I'd be there until I retired. Then Paris happened."

She was quiet for a couple of beats then she said, "At least you have a chance to get your memories back. Maybe when you can go to the Society and tell them what really happened in Paris...."

"They know all they need to know about that. I let a *satori* escape. In fact, I told her to stay away from the Society for her own good. That was all they needed to know to send me to Dearmont. Anything else is irrelevant to them."

"But not to you," Felicity said.

"Of course not. I want to know what the hell really happened in Paris and how I came to mail the Box of Midnight to myself. I don't appreciate having my memories erased by magic. I like things to be straightforward. The Blackwell sisters said there's a magical locked door in my mind, so my natural inclination is to open that door, whatever may be lurking behind it."

She nodded. "Yes, I suppose it's best to have everything out in the open." She sat back in her seat, a faraway look in her eyes, and I wondered if she was thinking about Jason again.

"You hungry?" I asked her. "There are meals in the kitchen. They're not great but they're filling if you eat two or three of them. You want something?" I got up and stood in the aisle, stretching my aching back and legs.

"Yes, please, but I think one will suffice, thanks."

"Coming up. And a coffee?"

"Cup of tea, please."

"Of course." I went up to the kitchen area, past the two guards who sat a few rows ahead of us. They still wore their shades despite being inside the plane.

In the kitchen, I took four TV dinners from the fridge and microwaved them one by one. Soon, the smell of chicken, beef, and vegetables drifted from the heated meals. I set them aside while I made a tea for Felicity and a coffee for myself.

Beyond the window, the sky was bright blue, the clouds floating below us like white puffs of whipped cream.

When I returned to the seats, balancing the hot meal trays on my arms while I held the drinks in my hands, Felicity was writing something on a slip of paper, copying it from her laptop.

I put her meal and drink on her seat tray and gave her a packet that contained a plastic knife and fork as well as salt and pepper. "If you want the meal to have much taste, you'll need the salt and pepper," I told her.

She waited until I'd sat down again, my three meals stacked on the seat next to me, before she handed me the slip of paper. "This is the magical formula you need to recite when you touch the statue of Hapi."

I looked at the hieroglyphs neatly lined up on the paper in Felicity's precise handwriting. The formula looked simple enough. I folded the paper and put it in my jeans pocket.

"This food isn't bad," Felicity said after tasting a mouthful of the chicken dinner I'd given her.

"You think?" I asked, tearing open sachets of salt and pepper and sprinkling them over the roast beef dinner I'd decided to eat first. "It's hardly a Darla's Double Burger. Now that is good food."

We ate in silence for a few minutes before she asked me, "Alec, can I ask you a personal question?"

"Sure," I said.

She hesitated before saying, "I was just wondering if you think our relationship goes beyond our working arrangement. What I mean is, are we friends?"

I wasn't sure exactly why she was asking that. When you go up against supernatural forces with someone, it tends to form a bond; you've both had a shared experience fighting a common enemy and, at its core, that's what friendship is about. Whether the fighting a common enemy means complaining about one of your teachers at high school or killing faerie changelings, it's all the same. It forms friendships. "Yes, I think we're friends. Don't you?"

She smiled. "Yes, of course we are. It's just that I've never really had any friends, so I wasn't sure. I was a geeky girl when I was growing up and I didn't really fit in. My parents made me socialize with the girls who lived on our street but while they were playing with dolls, I was looking at the books on their parents' bookshelves for something interesting to read. I've always been like that."

"I'm your friend," I said, "and I always will be. Even if you move back to England, we'll still be friends, Felicity. We spent time in the trenches together and that means a lot to me. And I'd say that Mallory and Leon are your friends too."

The smile grew until it lit up her face. "Thank you for saying that, Alec, it means a lot." Then the smile turned into a frown. "But it makes my decision much more difficult. When I moved over to America, the only people

85

I was leaving behind were my parents and Jason. I didn't see my parents much anyway, and I said I'd go back to visit them once a month or so. They were fine with that. And so was Jason, at first."

She pushed her meal aside. "What I'm trying to say is that it won't be so easy to leave Dearmont behind because for the first time in my life, I have friends."

"So don't leave," I suggested.

"It isn't that simple. On the other side of the ocean, there's Jason and a completely different sort of life. I'm torn."

"Let me tell you something," I said. "Every now and then, I look at the people who have no idea that the supernatural world exists and I envy them. I think to myself what a great life I might have had if I hadn't been thrown into this constant battle against creatures that most people think only exist in fairytales. But once you know about preternatural beings, once you know that magic is real and there are such things as enchanted swords and the faerie realm, you can't ever forget that. You and I, Felicity, we've seen things that most people will never see. And once you've seen those things, you can't turn your back on them, no matter how hard you try."

I hesitated, wondering if my speech made it sound like I was trying to talk her out of going back to Jason. I was trying to talk her out of it, but only because I knew how hard she would find leading a normal life when she had knowledge of the hidden things that exist in the world.

"What I'm trying to say is that your choice of whether to stay in Dearmont or move back to England is really a choice about who you are deep down inside. Are you the Felicity who helps protect mankind by assisting in preternatural investigations with the hope of one day becoming an investigator yourself, or are you the Felicity who leads a normal life married to a banker? You need to ask yourself if the latter option is even possible, knowing what you know about the world."

Her eyes filled with tears but they didn't spill down her cheeks, they just made her dark eyes glisten. "But if I leave Jason, I'll be leaving the only man I've ever loved, the only man who's ever loved me. He's my only link to a life of normality. If I throw that away, I'll be like a boat cast adrift in a dangerous sea. My life will be like yours, constantly uncovering murder and death wrought by supernatural monsters."

"It isn't all that bad," I said, defensively.

"No, I know that," she said, reaching across the aisle to touch my arm. Her hand was warm and she left it resting on my forearm as she spoke. "You know I want to be an investigator myself. Well, at least, I did want to be an investigator. Now, I'm not so sure."

"Working with me has put you off?" I asked. "If you want to be assigned to someone else, I can ask my father...."

"No, Alec, it isn't that. I don't want to work with anyone except you. It's just that this sudden trip to

London and being forced to make a decision has made me think long and hard about things. We see so much death. Poor George Robinson was killed by the changeling. Amy Cantrell had to see her own mother's dead body after it had risen from the grave. We're going to be investigating a church where people were most likely crushed to death by some creature or demon. I think about all that and I wonder how seeing it every day will change me. I don't want to become hardened to atrocities like that."

"You won't be," I said. "I'm not hardened to it and I've been working this job for years."

"But everyone has a different tolerance level. What you said is right; I'm not just deciding between Jason in England and my friends in America, I'm deciding who I want to be, what sort of life I want to live. That's why I'm torn. I don't think I know myself very well."

My eyes were drawn to the window beyond Felicity. Where there had been clear, bright sky only a moment ago, I could see dark blue storm clouds rolling toward the plane.

The seatbelt signs over every seat illuminated with a *ding*. The pilot's voice came over the speakers. "This is Captain Reynolds speaking. I've illuminated the fasten seatbelts signs so if you could all go ahead and do that, you'll be glad you did. We're experiencing some turbulence."

The plane rocked slightly.

"There's a storm approaching," Felicity said, buckling her seatbelt and staring out through her window.

"That's not a natural storm." I dug into my pocket and took out the crystal shard. Even before I removed it from the pouch, I could see that it was glowing a bright, icy blue. "We're under attack," I told Felicity.

"What?" She turned to face me and saw the glowing crystal. Her face went pale.

I unbuckled my seatbelt and stood up. My weekend bag was stowed beneath the seat behind me and my enchanted dagger was in there. I needed to get it.

"Alec, sit down," Felicity said. "Fasten your seat belt."

The plane tilted to the left at a sharp angle. I held onto my seat, but remained standing. "I need to get my dagger," I said.

Felicity looked from the storm-filled window to my face. "What? Why?"

"Because whatever's in that storm will be boarding this plane." I could hear the anxiety in my own voice. There was powerful magic at work to create a storm cloud of that size. The wielder of that magic might be inside the cloud and would soon be inside the plane. I hoped that whoever had cast the spell that created the cloud was elsewhere and was only sending lesser minions to kill us. Either way, I needed the dagger.

The pilot's voice came over the speakers again. "Mr, Harbinger, sit down!"

"We're being attacked," I shouted. I had no idea if he could hear me all the way at the front of the plane through the cockpit door, but at least the two goons in the suits and shades could. They were here to protect the plane and us, so it was time they did their job. "We need to lose altitude," I shouted as loudly as I could.

I wasn't sure if he had heard me and heeded my warning or if the air pressure within the storm forced the plane down, but we were suddenly dropping out of the sky. The emergency oxygen masks dropped from their hatches over the seats.

I began digging in my weekend bag, my hands reaching past my clothing to the dagger in its leather sheath. I unsheathed the weapon. It glowed bright blue in my hand as I struggled to regain my feet. The plane was still angled to the left and we were still descending fast. Thousands of feet below us was nothing but ocean and none of us were going to survive if we hit the water at this velocity.

The two guards didn't know what to do. They sat in their seats with their seatbelts fastened. I staggered along the aisle to where they were seated. They looked up at me, their eyes unreadable behind the shades.

"Are you guys armed?" I asked them.

They both nodded.

"Well, you should get your weapons ready, because we're about to be boarded."

The pilot must have regained control of the aircraft because our descent slowed slightly.

"Are you crazy?" the shaggy-haired one said. "Nothing's getting on this plane."

"Yeah," his bald partner agreed. "It's just a storm. It happens."

"It's a magical attack," I said, trying to keep my voice calm. "Do you have a crystal shard?"

"Yeah, I've got one here," Shaggy said, reaching into his jacket and pulling out a crystal shard that was glowing as brightly as the one I'd left on my seat. "Oh," he said. "We've got a problem."

Baldy looked at the shard and laughed dismissively. "Even if the storm is a magical attack, that doesn't mean anything's getting on this plane. The captain will handle it. He'll fly us to safety."

"The storm isn't the problem," I told him. "It's whatever is in the storm. Something is riding that cloud and coming this way." I had to grab the back of his seat when the plane jolted suddenly.

"Alec!" Felicity shouted.

I turned around and saw what had alarmed her. At the back of the plane, a portal was opening. It was a glowing red oval outlined by thick black smoke, large enough for a man to step through.

But what stepped through it and into the plane was no man.

91

CHAPTER 8

THE DEMON STOOD AT LEAST seven feet tall. Its skin was dark red and stretched tightly over thick muscles. Apart from the red skin, blazing yellow eyes, and black horns curled over its bald head, the demon looked humanoid, meaning it had two legs and two arms and only one head. Demons come in all shapes and sizes, and as things went, this one was less horrific than some I'd seen. It looked hideous, though, with sharp black claws at the tips of its fingers and equally sharp-looking teeth in its mouth that made its grin look shark-like.

It stepped forward, chattering its teeth together in a manner that was either supposed to scare us or was a signal to the second creature that came through the portal.

This demon was spider-like and it scuttled into the aisle between the seats like a huge tarantula. Despite its eight arachnid-like legs, it had a human head that was covered in the same hairy red skin as the rest of its body and had pure black eyes. It chattered its teeth in the same way the first demon had and I realized they were talking to each other in some hellish language. I had no idea what they were saying. Probably deciding which of us to kill first.

Felicity shrank back in her seat, her eyes full of fear. Behind me, the two guards had finally pulled their weapons, enchanted daggers like mine. The interior of the plane was illuminated blood red by the glowing portal with a hint of blue light emanating from our daggers.

The spider demon shot forward suddenly, shrieking in a high-pitched voice that made my teeth hurt. I dodged its charge, diving onto the seats next to me. As the demon passed by me, I lashed out with the dagger, slicing the enchanted blade through one of the scuttling legs. The shriek raised a couple of octaves as the demon's brain registered the damage I'd done to it. Dark green blood spurted from the wound, hitting the wall of the plane.

The creature charged into Shaggy, who lashed out with his own dagger, cutting through another of the demon's legs. More blood spurted, this time covering the opposite wall. When its foul stench reached my nose, I gagged. The smell was so bad it made my eyes water.

While the two guards fought the spider demon, I stepped back into the aisle to face the big red guy. It grinned with his shark-like mouth as I stood in front of it. "Stupid human," it said in a deep, throaty voice. "You are already dead and you don't even realize it. Our mission is already accomplished."

I didn't know what the hell it was talking about until a chill shot through the air and I heard a rushing sound all around me. I glanced at the walls on either side of me and cursed. The plane walls were disappearing where the spider demon's blood had touched them. The blood must have been some kind of acid; the sides of the plane were melting away, exposing us to the freezing air outside. As the cabin lost pressure, I felt the air being ripped out of my lungs.

The red-skinned demon laughed and showed me his sharp black claws. "I will end you now. These other humans can die in the crash, but your death, Harbinger, must be reported to my masters. There must be no doubt that you are gone." He lunged forward, swiping his claws at me. I managed to step back out of the way, bringing the dagger up to defend myself. The demon skillfully avoided the blade.

Behind me, one of the guards screamed. The sound was cut off almost as soon as it had begun and became a low gurgling. Beyond the windows, the clouds parted to reveal the shimmering surface of the sea below. The plane juddered as the captain applied the air brakes in an attempt to slow our descent.

He was doing his best but he needed to get us to a lower altitude so we didn't freeze to death or suffocate when all the air escaped.

I leapt at the big red demon, more out of desperation than skill, and plunged the glowing dagger into its chest. A strong smell of sulfur erupted from the wound. The blade ripped through the tight red skin and cut into the muscle beneath. I'd been hoping to hit the creature's heart but I had no idea where this monster's heart was situated in its body.

With a tight grip on the hilt of the dagger, I pulled the blade down, hoping to cause as much damage to the demon as I could before it killed me. If the guards killed the spider thing and I damaged this one enough to get it to flee back though the portal, Felicity might have a chance of survival if the pilot did his job correctly and managed to crash land the plane on the water.

The demon roared with pain and anger, thrusting its hand up to grab me by the throat and lift me into the air. My back hit the aircraft's ceiling. What little air had been in my lungs was gone and I felt blackness closing in from all sides. I was dimly aware of the dagger in my hand. I waved it weakly at the demon. The hellish creature grinned. "Now you must die, Harbinger." It brought back its other hand, sharp claws ready to tear into me.

Then the blazing yellow eyes went wide and the sharp-toothed grin became a gasp of surprise. The demon's grip faltered and I struggled out of its grasp as I saw the glowing blue point of an enchanted sword cut through the creature's chest. The sword was withdrawn and the demon fell to the floor.

Felicity stood behind it, the sword glowing in her hand, her dark eyes wide as she looked down at the creature she had just impaled.

The demon wasn't dead. It sprang to its feet and swept a clawed hand at Felicity, throwing her almost the entire length of the plane. She landed near the swirling red and black portal, the sword lying at her feet, its glow dying.

I tried to temper my rage at the demon and control my next attack, but my emotions took over and I leapt at it, slashing and stabbing the dagger over and over. It staggered backward as I drove the dagger into its body over and over; I ignored the stench of brimstone coming from the damned creature and concentrating only on killing the damned thing. I had to get to Felicity and make sure she was okay.

Finally, the demon lay dead beneath me. I climbed off its corpse before the flames that erupted over its skin caught my clothes. While the body burned and filled the plane with a vile odor, I ran to Felicity and crouched over her unmoving body. The left side of her white blouse was torn, revealing a bloody wound beneath.

"Felicity," I said, "are you okay?"

Her eyes fluttered open. "Alec? What happened?"

A sigh of relief escaped my already oxygen-starved lungs. "You helped me fight a demon," I said.

"That's good," she said weakly. Her eyes closed again.

Her wound needed attention. She was losing blood. I went in search of a first aid kit.

At the front of the plane, the spider demon's body was on fire, the same as the big red demon's. The heat singed the carpet on the floor. Baldy was standing near the body, sweat beading on his head. Shaggy was dead, lying face down in a pool of the demon's green acidic blood. The acid was eating through Shaggy's body and the floor beneath him. The portal that had formed at the rear of the plane was gone.

The plane rumbled. Through the windows and the melted parts of the fuselage, I could see that we were only a couple of hundred feet above the sea now. The pilot had managed to get us to a lower altitude but the aircraft felt unsteady beneath my feet.

"First-aid kit!" I shouted at Baldy. "Where is it?"

"Back there," he said, pointing to a curtained area at the rear of the plane. He seemed to be in shock and I wasn't sure I could blame him. Acid-spewing demons were beyond the limits of anyone's job description.

I went to the curtain and pulled it back to reveal a stash of weapons and shelves of medical supplies. At least the Society equipped their planes for emergencies. This must be where Felicity had found the sword she'd used to stab the demon. Maybe she'd been hoping to hide behind the curtain, then found the weapon and decided to fight.

I grabbed bandages, cotton balls, and a bottle of antiseptic and took them over to where she lay. Cleaning the blood off her skin with antiseptic-soaked cotton balls, I inspected the ragged cut that stretched from her hip to her ribs. It didn't look too deep but I knew that demon scratches were sometimes poisonous and that the poison could cause anything from death to a few days of illness, depending on the demon. All I could do was bandage the wound and hope for the best. Felicity needed proper medical treatment at a Society hospital where they knew how to deal with demon poison, but right now, that was impossible. We were in the middle of the Atlantic Ocean, thousands of miles from anywhere.

I wrapped the bandages around Felicity's midriff and tied them off.

The speakers crackled and the pilot shouted, "Brace yourselves!"

I picked Felicity up and carried her to the nearest seat. After buckling her seat belt, I took the seat next to hers and fastened myself into it. I put my arm across Felicity's chest, holding her steady in the seat. Her eyes flickered open for a few seconds and then closed again. She was in the grip of the demon's poison.

The plane's engines began to whine as the pilot applied the air brakes again in an attempt to slow us down before impact. When we hit, the underside of the plane skimmed the sea and cold water sprayed into the cabin through the gaps where the fuselage had melted. The tang of salty water filled the air, dispelling the sulfurous odor that had lingered there before. The floor vibrated beneath my boots as the ocean created friction against the aircraft's undercarriage. A loud rushing sound filled the air and it was so loud that it overwhelmed my senses. It scattered all my thoughts as it filled my head. It was like being inside a huge washing machine. The plane lurched as it plunged into the sea. Cold ocean water began rushing in through the holes in the fuselage, covering my boots and Felicity's shoes. Even the chill of the water on her feet didn't wake her.

The engines roared a final time and then died. There was no sound now other than the lapping of the waves against the plane and the rush of the water filling the cabin.

I unbuckled myself and Felicity, throwing her over my shoulder and splashing through the water in the aisle, moving forward to where Baldy sat. He looked up at me and said flatly, "We're alive."

"We won't be if we don't get off this damn plane," I told him.

The cockpit door opened and the pilot and co-pilot, both dressed in neat white shirts and black trousers, came into the cabin. The pilot was an older man with salt and pepper hair and a moustache that made him look like he belonged in a World War II fighter plane. "I'm Captain Reynolds," he said. "Let's get out of here." He and the co-pilot, a much younger fair-haired man, went to the rear of the plane and opened the door there before throwing the life raft through it.

"Life jackets are under the seats," Reynolds said. "I suggest you wear one."

I wasn't about to argue. I put Felicity down in the nearest seat and dug around until I found two life jackets. I put one on her and pulled the cord to inflate it.

"Don't inflate them until we get out of the plane," Reynolds told me.

"Unless you didn't notice," I said, "the water is inside the plane." It had risen almost to my knees. We were sinking fast.

Baldy went to the weapon room and began stuffing swords, daggers, and crossbows into canvas bags. That must be procedure in case of emergency. The enchanted weapons were too valuable to lose to the sea.

I carried Felicity to the open door. The life raft was inflated and waiting, the co-pilot sitting inside it and doing his best to keep it close to the plane. "Pass me the girl," he offered.

"I'll hold onto her," I said, stepping onto the raft with Felicity over my shoulder.

Baldy appeared at the door and tossed the bags of weapons into the raft. They rattled and clinked as they landed on the floor of the raft. Baldy followed them, making the raft shake as he landed inside it. At least his shades were still intact.

"Everyone okay?" Reynolds asked before stepping onto the raft and nodding to his co-pilot. The young man started a small outboard motor and drove us away from the sinking aircraft.

"Blankets for the lady," Reynolds said, handing me a bundle of blankets. I placed them over Felicity's sleeping form and sat close to share my body heat with her. Not that I had much body heat to share; I was cold and wet and my salt-stained clothes clung to me like an uncomfortable second skin.

"What the hell happened?" the co-pilot asked.

"We were attacked by demons," I said. "Whoever sent that storm had some pretty powerful magic. Opening a portal on board a moving plane is a very complex work of sorcery."

"Any ideas who it might be?" Reynolds asked. Then he held up his hands. "Never mind, I know you couldn't tell us even if you knew. We're just the hired help. Still, I'd like to know who destroyed my aircraft." He looked across the waves to where the plane had almost completely sunk. Only the nose was above water and that was sinking fast as well. Reynolds sighed. "Goodbye, old girl."

"How long until the Society rescues us?" I asked him.

He consulted an electronic device that was encased in black and yellow rubber. "Well, judging by how far we were from the coast when I sent the distress signal, I'd say we've got maybe six or seven hours on this dingy before we're rescued. Our best bet is if there's an aircraft carrier in the area. The Society will radio the Navy to send a helicopter our way to pick us up."

"They can do that?" I wasn't sure why I was so surprised that the Society of Shadows could order the

Royal Navy to rescue us; the Society had been around for centuries and some of its members moved in powerful social circles.

"Of course," he said. "So we just have to wait until someone comes along to rescue us." He made himself comfortable against the side of the raft, folded his arms, and closed his eyes as if being forced out of the sky by demons and ending up on a life raft was an everyday occurrence for him.

"One thing's for sure, Harbinger," Baldy said; "Somebody wants you dead real bad."

I'd been thinking the same thing myself. The red demon had known my name and said that my death had to be confirmed to its master. It wasn't enough for it to simply crash the plane; it had to make sure there was no way I could survive.

Whoever had the Staff of Midnight wanted me dead, that was for sure, and that person had sent assassins after me before, but nothing on this scale. Maybe I was on someone else's shit list as well and I was the target of not one, but two powerful magicians. Great, that was just what I needed.

There was nothing I could do about it out here in the middle of the Atlantic, so I settled back against the inflatable wall of the raft and adjusted the blankets that covered Felicity. Her breathing was slow and deep, as if she were sleeping. I hoped her dreams were pleasant and not nightmares of the horror she'd just faced.

Taking my cue from Reynolds, I closed my eyes and listened to the waves slapping against the side of the life raft.

* * *

It was almost three hours later when I heard a helicopter in the distance. At first, I thought I was imagining the distant sound, but the high-pitched hum got louder and when I opened my eyes, I could see a dark shape in the sky.

Reynolds grabbed a red flare from the raft's supply box and lit it, waving it above his head to get the helicopter's attention.

I checked on Felicity. She was still lying in the same position, breathing deeply and slowly. I guessed that the poison in the red demon's claws was of the type that made a human sick for a few days. If it was the fatal type, I was sure Felicity would be dead by now. At least, I had to believe that. If she had been fatally wounded because someone wanted to kill me and she just happened to be in the wrong place at the wrong time, I would never forgive myself.

The helicopter hovered above us, its blades chopping the air noisily and causing a downdraft that made the sea around us ripple outward in tiny waves. I held the blankets tight around Felicity so they wouldn't blow away.

A man in a white helmet and blue flight suit descended on a cable until his booted feet touched the raft. The name

"Reynolds" was sewn on the left breast of the flight suit. "I've got four survivors," he said into the mic on the helmet, presumably to the pilot in the helicopter. Looking at us, he said, "I don't know who you people are, but you must be very important to someone. Our naval aircraft carrier was rerouted to carry out a search and rescue mission as a priority. And there's a chopper *en route* from the mainland to pick you up from our ship."

"He's the important one," the captain said, pointing at me.

"No," I said, indicating Felicity. "She's the important one. She needs medical attention."

Reynolds nodded. "We'll get all of you back to our ship ASAP. We've got a good medical team on board."

I shook my head. "The only people who can help her are the people coming from the mainland in that helicopter." I knew the Society would send a medical team to collect us and that team would have knowledge of demon poison. The Navy medics in the ship we were headed to now would be baffled.

"Well, they shouldn't take too long to get here," Reynolds said. He held out a nylon harness. "Okay, who wants to go for a ride first?"

"She does," I said, pointing at Felicity.

Reynolds nodded. "No problem."

Later, when we were all on board the naval helicopter and heading for the ship, I looked back at the empty life raft, an insignificant speck in the shimmering ocean.

Somebody wanted me dead, and they were willing to bring down a plane to achieve that goal. The thing was, I was pretty sure it wasn't the person who had the Staff of Midnight. After all, if they knew I was on a plane bound for London, why bother trying to kill me at all? Why not just go to Dearmont and grab the box? If the staff could guide them to the box, then they had to know it was in Maine and that I didn't have it, so going to such a huge effort to kill me would be pointless.

No, whoever had crashed our plane wanted me dead for some other reason.

For some reason, I wasn't only important to the Society of Shadows; I was important to the bad guys, too. And I had no idea why.

As we got farther away from the crash site, the tiny speck that had been our life raft vanished among the gray expanse of the sea.

CHAPTER 9

IT WAS ALMOST TEN IN the evening, London time, when a black Bentley dropped me off outside a large building near Hyde Park. The tall building's only identifying feature was a gold plaque that read MYSTERIUM IMPORT AND EXPORT on the wall next to the heavy wooden doors. I always wondered if using the Latin word for mysterious as part of the Society's cover was some kind of inside joke. I pressed the button on the intercom next to the door and looked up into the camera mounted above it, knowing that a facial recognition program was attempting to identify me right now, and I was being checked out by the building's magical wards.

A heavy click told me that the doors had unlocked. I pushed through them and stood in a grand marbled lobby that certainly didn't belong to any import and export company. Walking into the Society's headquarters was like stepping back in time to the Victorian era. Although the Society moved with the times and was just as tech-savvy as any other organization, its outward appearance spoke of antiquity and a bygone age. Portraits hung on the walls that followed a wide, curving staircase up to the upper levels. The walls themselves were dark and wood-paneled. A rich yet subtle scent of smoky wood hung in the air and I was sure it was part of the outer illusion of age, probably emanating from incense in the ventilation system.

A large, curved, wooden reception desk was situated by the door and there were two men and a woman, dressed impeccably in dark gray suits and a dark gray dress respectively, working behind it. I had no doubt that if, despite the camera and wards, someone got into the building who didn't belong, these three would be more than capable of taking care of the problem.

One of the men smiled at me as if he were the receptionist at a hotel and I was here to check in. "Mr. Harbinger. It's good to have you back with us. I trust your journey was a pleasant one?"

"Not really. I was in a plane crash, then I spent an hour on an aircraft carrier waiting for helicopter to bring me to the mainland. Then I spent two more hours in the car you sent to collect me from the airfield worrying about my friend who's been taken to the hospital."

His smile never faltered. "I'm sorry to hear that, sir. Your father is expecting you. I'll get George here to escort you to his office."

"I know where it is," I said, walking toward the bank of elevators across the room.

"You know the policy, sir." He looked at this colleague. "George, would you escort Mr. Harbinger to his father's office, please?"

George, a dark-haired man who looked like he was all muscles and steroids beneath his suit, nodded and came out from behind the desk. "This way, sir." He led me to the elevators and pressed the button to call one.

Yeah, I knew the policy of this place. Nobody was allowed to go anywhere without an escort, and that included the preternatural investigators. In fact, the policy had probably been put in place specifically to stop P.I.s from wandering around the place. As far as the Society's ranking system went, we were on the bottom rung of the ladder. And it wasn't a ladder I wanted to climb either; I was happy enough out in the field. I'd probably go crazy if I had to work in a stuffy office and deal with politics and social niceties.

The only downside to being one of the Society's drones was that I had to be escorted around the building like a naughty child.

The elevator took us to the fifth floor where George led me along a wood-paneled corridor to a door bearing a plaque that read THOMAS HARBINGER. He knocked and waited until my father's voice said, "Enter," before opening the door and ushering me inside.

I went into the office, which looked like a cozy library in an old house more than a place of work. Stuffed bookshelves covered every wall, floor to ceiling, except where a large stone fireplace had been built into one wall. In front of the fireplace were two leather armchairs, each with its own side table upon which sat a lamp with a dark green glass shade. The fire was lit and crackling gently.

An old desk sat at the far end of the room, covered in papers and books and, the one item here that confirmed I hadn't actually stepped into the past, a computer. My father, who had been sitting behind the desk, grinned when he saw me and came over to greet me.

He looked a little more tired than the last time I'd seen him, but I guessed he had been worrying about his son being involved in a plane accident. Or maybe not. There was probably some aspect of the job keeping him up late.

He wore a dark green suit and tie over his robust frame and he was as well-groomed as always, his gray beard trimmed close to his cheeks and chin, his hair neatly combed and cut. The tiredness was in his gray eyes, which were a little bloodshot and didn't shine with their usual spark of clarity.

"Alec," he said, spreading his arms and coming in for a hug, "how are you?"

"I've been better," I said as we embraced.

"Yes, I heard about what happened. Terrible business. At least you're here safely."

"I can't say the same for Felicity," I said, breaking away from the hug.

"She'll be fine, Son. I've heard from the hospital that the poison was mild and she'll sleep it off in a couple of days."

I let out a slow breath of relief. During the drive here, my anxiety over Felicity's health had slowly built until it had become a tight knot in my gut. Now, that knot unraveled slightly.

"Do you know who attacked the plane?" I asked.

He nodded. "I have a good idea. Let's have a drink and talk about it. Scotch?" He went to a wooden cabinet and opened it to reveal a bar stocked with an assortment of liquor bottles and glasses.

"I could use a beer," I said.

His face fell slightly. "I'm afraid I only have spirits here."

"Scotch is fine." I took a seat by the fire, my eyes roaming over the imposing bookshelves. Most of the books were on occult subjects, in many different languages. I saw some French and Latin titles I recognized and knew that if they were in my father's library, they were first editions.

He came over with the drinks and sat in the chair facing me. "How are things in Dearmont?"

I shrugged. "I'm working in a couple of cases."

"Anything interesting?"

"You wouldn't think so. I'm sure they aren't as exciting as running the organization." I took a sip of the scotch. It burned as it slid down my throat. It was definitely the good stuff, though.

"I don't run it alone, Alec, you know that. I'm just a cog in a big wheel."

I arched an eyebrow at that. As cogs went, he was an integral one, as far as I knew.

"I sometimes miss my days in the field," he said before taking a drink. "The work seemed more ... honest. I have to deal with politics now, where you only have to fight monsters." He grinned and added, "Perhaps those two things are actually quite similar."

I smiled but I wanted him to get to the point. I wanted to know why I'd been summoned here in the first place and who he thought had attacked the plane. As soon as I had that information, I was going to get a cab to the hospital so I could visit Felicity. Anything beyond that didn't interest me. I didn't give a damn about political in-fighting among the Society's upper classes.

"So," I said, "why am I here, Dad?"

"You always were one who liked to get straight to the point," he said. "I suppose I should explain why I called you here."

"Well, I know it wasn't for a father-and-son chat," I said.

He gave me a thin-lipped smile. "No, it's business."

"I didn't expect anything else."

He sighed. "Fair enough, I'll get straight to the point. Have you ever heard of an organization called the Midnight Cabal?"

"Yeah, of course. They were a secret group of occultists. They were around in the seventeenth century, weren't they?"

He nodded. "The Midnight Cabal is as old as the Society of Shadows. When the Society was formed, it pledged to protect humanity from the monsters in this world. The Cabal had the opposite goal. They were bent on the destruction of mankind and a return to the Dark Ages, when magic and superstition held sway over everyone from farmers to royalty."

"So it's a good thing the Cabal vanished two hundred years ago," I said. The serious look he gave me over his glass of scotch told me everything I needed to know. "They didn't vanish, did they." I said. It was more a statement than a question.

"They seemed to have vanished," he said. "As far as the history books are concerned, the Midnight Cabal disappeared entirely around the year 1745 or so. However, it seems that they simply went underground. Just like everyone else, the Society thought the Cabal was gone, but we now know that they still exist today. They've been biding their time, making plans to destroy the Society of Shadows and all of mankind and throw the world into darkness."

"So they sent those demons to attack the plane because it belonged to the Society?"

"I would say that's a fair assumption," he said.

"One of those demons knew my name," I said.

His face paled. "What?"

"It called me Harbinger and said that my death had to be confirmed to its masters."

My father put his drink on the side table, in the pool of lamplight. He stared into the fire for a moment, frowning.

"What's going on?" I asked him. "You seem to know something about this that I don't."

"Are you sure the demon called you by your name?" His eyes didn't look so tired now. Instead, they looked worried.

"Yeah, I'm positive." I could have added that I'd already been the target of an attempted assassination by ogres and a hitman named Tunnock, but I kept that to myself. My father didn't know I had a magical box that could raise the dead, or that someone was gunning for me because of it. He wasn't the only one who could keep secrets. "So are you going to tell me why the demon knowing my name has you so worried?"

He turned his face to me and smiled. "I'm just worried for you, Alec. Can't a father be worried about his son?"

I was pretty sure it was more than that, and the fact that the worried look remained in his eyes told me I was right. "Okay," I said, sighing. There was no point pursuing this; if he wanted to keep something from me, there was nothing I could do to convince him otherwise. "So you flew me all the way here to tell me about the Midnight Cabal. They're still around. Got it. I'll be on the lookout for Cabal members in Dearmont just as soon as I get back there. I'm sure they'll be more interested in a place like Dearmont than, say, oh, I don't know, New York."

He frowned at me. "There's no need for sarcasm, Alec. The discovery of the Midnight Cabal makes your loss of the *satori* in Paris even more disastrous. She would have been a great help to us in these troubled times."

"I didn't lose her, Dad, I let her get away."

"That makes it even worse. And we aren't exactly sure what happened, are we? Because the *satori* wiped your memory of most of it."

I didn't have a sarcastic comeback for that because he was right. Some of my memories of Paris had been taken and replaced with false ones. I had a vague recollection of going to the catacombs, finding the *satori* there, and telling her to run from the Society because I knew there was some sort of corruption within the organization. But bits and pieces of the timeline were missing. Devon Blackwell had told me that there was a magically-locked door in my mind and the memories must be behind it. Unless Felicity's plan regarding the statue at the museum worked, I had no idea how to open that door and recover what had been stolen from me.

"Anyway, let's not go over old ground," my father said. "There isn't much point when you can't remember any of it. But the reason I called you here is in regards to what happened in Paris. We may have lost the *satori* but I gained some valuable information regarding the Paris investigators. Pierre was right when he said they were traitors. Most of them were found dead in the Paris catacombs but some have gone missing. I fear they may have been working for the Midnight Cabal."

I thought about that for a moment. "Okay, I guess that makes sense. If any organization is likely to infiltrate the Society and work its evil from the inside, it'll be our oldest enemy."

He leaned forward and lowered his voice. "I believe I know who those French investigators were secretly working for. I had the Coven do some magical digging and their spells led them to a member of the Inner Circle, a man named John DuMont. Alec, you understand that everything I am telling you is in strictest confidence and not to be repeated to anyone, not even other members of the Society."

"Yeah, I got that with the whole traitor thing. I have two questions." I whispered, "Why are you telling me this and what is the Coven?"

"I'm telling you because, as my son, you are the only person I can trust. I need you to do something for me. I can't ask anyone else in case they're working for DuMont. If he was able to get to the Paris investigators, there's no doubt he controls others in the Society, probably even members here in London."

That made sense. If a member of the Inner Circle was responsible for the corruption within the Society, then it probably spread far and wide. "And the Coven?" I asked.

He looked at me and pursed his lips as if deciding how much to tell me.

"Hey," I said, "I'm the person you trust, remember?"

He considered that and then nodded slowly. "Very well. Come with me and I'll show you the Coven." He stood and started toward the door before stopping and turning to face me. "Alec, again, I have to tell you that this is strictly…."

"Yeah, I know, confidential. Either you trust me or you don't, Dad. You can't have it both ways." I followed him to the door.

"I trust you, Alec," he said as we left his office and walked toward the elevators. "The Coven is, as the name implies, a group of witches situated within this building. There are nine of them, and together, they provide the enchantments and spells the Society needs to function. To fight magical creatures, we sometimes need to use magic of our own." He stepped into the elevator and took a key from his pocket. Inserting the key into the elevator control panel, he pressed a series of buttons. The doors closed and we began to descend.

"The witches discovered that John DuMont is most likely a traitor, after I asked them to look into the matter."

"And you trust the Coven?" I asked.

"It isn't a matter of trust. These nine witches are the real Society of Shadows. They banded together in 1682 to fight malevolent supernatural beings and protect mankind. They called themselves the Society of Shadows. Everything you think of as the Society—this building, the investigators, the Inner Circle, the cases—has been built around the witches over the centuries. But they are the organization's core. They are the source of its power."

The floor indicator above the door dropped down to B for basement, then went blank. We were still descending.

"They're underground?" I asked. "Beneath the headquarters basement?"

My father shook his head. "Not really. They don't exist in an actual physical location beneath the basement, if that's what you mean. They don't exist in our world at all anymore. They died centuries ago but they now exist in an otherworldly place."

"And this elevator can take us there," I mused.

"I don't know exactly how it works," he said, "Nor do I care to."

We came to a halt. I waited for the doors to open, curious to see the witches who had formed the Society of Shadows over three centuries ago. The doors remained closed.

"It takes a while," my father said. "We're shifting into their realm of existence."

A couple of minutes later, the door slid open, revealing a passageway hewn out of rock. Although there were no torches to light the passageway, a dim glow seemed to emanate from the rock walls. The air was warm and smelled of cedarwood and lotus flower.

"This way," my dad said, stepping out of the elevator and striding along the passageway. I followed him to the end of the passageway where a set of stone stairs spiraled down further into the earth. The same glow lit the wide stone steps.

We descended slowly until we reached a small area at the foot of the stairs where a rough archway had been cut in the rock. Beyond the archway, there appeared to be nothing but impenetrable blackness.

I reached into my jacket and took out the mini Maglite I always carried.

"You won't need that," my father said. "The darkness is a magical barrier set into the archway. It will let us through and there's light beyond it." Her stepped into the archway and disappeared into the blackness.

Putting the flashlight away, I followed and felt a slight tingling all over my body as I stepped through the archway and into a large circular cavern that was lit with the same dim glow as the passageway. Stalactites hung from the high ceiling and stalagmites rose from the floor here and there, but most of the floor was laid with granite flagstones. They widened into an area where nine cowled figures knelt around a circular pool. The figures' faces were shrouded in shadow.

My father stepped forward and I followed. There was a hum of energy in the cavern, like an electrical storm building power before shooting lightning to earth. We reached the pool, which I could now see didn't contain water at all but a jet black fluid that writhed and flowed sinuously.

The nine figures didn't look up. They continued to gaze at the inky black pool.

"I've brought my son," my father said to nobody in particular. "He's going to help us with the DuMont matter."

A soft, feminine voice said, "The boy has become a man. He will assist us well."

The voice seemed not to be coming from any of the cowled figures but from the pool itself.

A second voice, also emanating from the pool in soft, dulcet tones, said, "He will assist us well, but the door will be unlocked."

A third, similar voice replied, "Yes, but it is perhaps time."

I whispered to my dad, "What are they talking about?"

He silenced me with a glare.

A fourth voice said, "The dead shall rise."

In reply, a fifth voice answered, "A difficult decision must be made."

"The curse of the heart," said a sixth voice.

"Blood must be spilled, despite the consequences," said a seventh.

"All will be lost and all will be gained," an eighth voice said.

The ninth said, "These things may come to pass or they may not. Nothing is certain."

"Can you see my future?" I asked them.

"We see a future."

"Whether it shall come to pass depends on many things. A thread can unravel in an infinite variety of ways."

"What can you tell us about John DuMont?" my father asked.

"The traitor shall be among the dead tomorrow at midnight."

"Beneath the Cedar of Lebanon."

"Beware the undead."

"Strike their hearts."

"The door may be already open."

"A flood of memory."

"Our work shall be undone."

"Perhaps it is time."

"These things may come to pass or they may not. Nothing is certain."

I sighed. "Are they always this cryptic?"

"Alec, be quiet!" my father said in a low, angry tone. To the witches, he asked, "Is there anything more you can tell us?"

"The thread will unravel when the time is right."

"The box."

"The staff."

"The hour."

"Three things of midnight."

"The Cabal makes four."

"A time of darkness."

"A time to weep."

"These things may come to pass or they may not. Nothing is certain."

We waited for a few moments longer but the witches said nothing more. My father tapped me in the shoulder and nodded toward the way we'd come in. We left. As we walked back the way we had come, I went over the witches' words in my head. Some of what they'd said was obvious, such as the box and the staff.

I assumed the curse of the heart referred to the curse attached to the Box of Midnight but wondered if it might mean the situation between Mallory and me. That was a curse of the heart if ever there was one. It might even refer to Felicity having to leave a job she loved to be with Jason. That was the trouble with prophecy; it was always so damned enigmatic.

I reminded myself that I hadn't come here for a fortune-telling session, merely to meet the Coven. At least they'd told us where John DuMont would be tomorrow at midnight.

"Did you get the clue?" my dad asked as we entered the elevator. "The Cedar of Lebanon?"

"Of course. It's the big old tree in Highgate Cemetery, the one above the circle of crypts called the Circle of Lebanon."

He put his key into the panel and hit the sequence of buttons that would take us back to our own realm. "Good lad. So we're going to have to make our plans before we go there tomorrow at midnight."

"We? Dad, I think your days in the field are long past."

"Nonsense. I'm just as capable as I've always been."

I arched an eyebrow and gave him an "are you sure?" look.

"I'm fine," he said.

"I think there's going to be vampires there. One of the witches said to beware the undead and another told us to strike their hearts. That's the best way of killing vampires that I know of, a stake through the heart."

"Yes, you're probably right."

"So get me a team of investigators and we'll go there armed to the teeth with stakes. There's no need for you to come."

"I told you, I can't trust anyone. I don't know who's working with DuMont and who isn't. I can't send you to Highgate Cemetery with a group of investigators who will kill you as soon as you arrive."

"There must be someone you trust in this organization."

"I trusted DuMont. He was a member of the Inner Circle. My trust was misplaced in him so I can't be sure that it isn't misplaced in others as well."

"Dad, I'd rather go to Highgate Cemetery alone than have to worry about your well-being while fighting DuMont. By the way, what is the actual plan when I confront him? Do you want me to kill him?"

"Good heavens, no! We need information from him, names of other traitors. He might even be able to lead us to the Midnight Cabal. There are a few different items we can use to capture him. I'll get a couple sorted out tomorrow."

"There's that 'we' again."

He sighed and punched in a new sequence of numbers on the elevator's control panel.

"What are you doing?"

"Taking you back to the lobby. We aren't going to argue about this, Alec, so you may as well leave and go to your hotel. I'll be there tomorrow night and we'll go to Highgate Cemetery together. That's my final word on the subject."

I shook my head at his stubbornness. There was no point arguing. The elevator doors opened onto the lobby.

"Do you have a vehicle?" my dad asked.

"No, I'm going to get a cab."

"No need for that." He shouted to the front desk, "George, get my son a vehicle from the garage. You prefer Land Rovers don't you?" he asked me.

I nodded.

"A Land Rover," he told George.

"Of course, sir," George replied.

I stepped out of the elevator and walked toward the desk.

"Tomorrow, Alec," my father said from behind me.

"Yeah, tomorrow."

As if facing DuMont and a bunch of vampires wasn't already going to be bad enough, now I had to do it with my father in tow.

CHAPTER 10

THE HOSPITAL WHERE FELICITY HAD been admitted was situated on the bank of the River Thames, overlooking expensive riverfront properties with a view of the Parliament Buildings farther downriver. I found her room after being told at the front desk which ward she was in. It was a regular, mundane hospital, but the Society owned a couple of wards, and employed a compliment of private doctors and nurses that had received training at the Academy of Shadows as well as their usual medical qualifications.

I went up to the ward in the elevator, holding a bouquet of flowers I'd bought at the shop downstairs. The bouquet consisted mainly of hyacinths and daffodils in bright spring colors. It would add a little color to Felicity's room and hopefully cheer her up when she regained consciousness.

On the ward, a nurse asked to see my I.D. before she'd let me see Felicity. I obliged, showing her my P.I. card, and was shown to the open door of a room. I thanked the nurse and went inside.

The lights had been turned down low. Felicity was lying in the bed with her eyes closed, an IV tube snaking out of one arm. She looked peaceful and her pulse and oxygen levels, displayed on the machines by the bed, were normal.

I felt relieved that she was in good hands now, as far as medical care went, and she seemed to be doing okay.

"You must be Alec Harbinger," said a male voice from the shadows by the bed.

I started, almost dropping the flowers. A young man with neat, short hair, and dressed in a shirt and tie, got up out of the chair next to the bed and came over to me, hand outstretched. "I'm Jason Farmer, Felicity's partner."

We shook. He had a weak grip and I felt like I was crushing his hand with my own, stronger handshake, so I made it brief.

"You're the person she worked for," Jason said. "The investigator of the supernatural." There was a definite note of disdain in his voice and I noted his use of the past tense.

I placed the flowers gently on the table by the bed. "That's me," I said.

"So can you tell me what happened to Felicity?"

"What did the doctors tell you?"

"That she was in a plane crash and she suffered a concussion."

"Then that's what happened."

He didn't seem satisfied with that answer. He pointed his finger at me in a manner that was probably supposed to be threatening but failed miserably. Jason was thin and weedy. He was nothing like the muscled Adonis I'd imagined whenever Felicity had mentioned him. "Look, I have a right to know what happened to my girlfriend. Just because she went gallivanting off to America doesn't mean you can hide things from me. I know there's more to this than meets the eye."

"Did the doctors say she's going to be okay?" I asked him.

He dropped his finger. "Yes, in a day or two."

"Then that's all you need to be concerned about. She's going to be fine." I turned to leave. It was getting too stuffy all of a sudden and I needed air.

"It isn't only her physical state I'm worried about," Jason said. "I know you've been filling her head with crazy nonsense."

"What?" I turned to face him.

"You know what I'm talking about. Every time I called her she was like a giddy schoolgirl, telling me how she loved her job and that little nowhere town. She told me you were helping her put in the time she needed to be an investigator herself. I don't know what the hell you think you're doing, but Felicity doesn't belong over there. You're making things worse by telling her she could be an investigator, too, filling her head with crazy ideas."

"She could be an investigator," I said evenly. I wasn't going to let this guy rile me. "That isn't crazy."

"Of course it is. She belongs here with me."

"Maybe she can decide that for herself."

He snorted. "She doesn't know what she wants most of the time."

"We're done here," I said, turning toward the door.

He grabbed my arm. "Listen," he said. "Tell her you can't take her back. Make her stay here and put all these silly notions of being an investigator out of her head." He reached inside his trouser pocket and pulled out a black leather wallet. "If it's money you need…."

I swatted the wallet out of his hand. It went flying across the room and slapped against the wall. Then I shook him off me a little more vigorously than necessary and he stumbled backward, landing on his ass.

"Don't ever speak to me again," I told him before walking out into the corridor.

When I got outside, I took in a lungful of the night air and let it out slowly, trying to stay calm. Felicity was going to be okay, that was what mattered. I just had to hold onto that thought and not give in to the urge to go back up there and throw Jason out of the window.

I wasn't ready to go to the hotel yet; I needed to move, to let off the pent-up anger I felt building inside me.

Instead of going to the parking lot, I headed for the wide path that followed the bank of the Thames.

As I walked beneath the dull glow of the streetlights, the river dark and mysterious beside me, I pulled up the collar of my jacket and stuffed my hands into my pockets.

The night had become suddenly cold.

CHAPTER 11

THE FOLLOWING MORNING, I WOKE up in my hotel room to the sound of rain drumming on the windows. Sliding out of bed and pulling back the curtains, I looked out over the gray city. It was a good day to visit the museum. I had nothing else to do until tonight, when I was going on a hunting trip in the cemetery with my dad, so I might as well touch the ancient statue and recite the formula Felicity had given me.

I took the scrap of paper out of my jeans pocket and looked at the hieroglyphs she had written down in five neat rows. These simple characters could be the key to unlocking the memories the *satori* had put behind a door in my mind. Speaking the sounds that each hieroglyph represented softly, I was satisfied I could do what was required to work the magic of the statue.

After calling the hospital and being told by a nurse that Felicity was in the same condition as last night, I showered and dressed and went down to the hotel's restaurant for breakfast.

Two hours later, I decided to leave the Land Rover in the hotel parking lot and hail a cab. It was easier to get around London in a cab or on the London Underground and many people who lived here didn't even own cars. However, the Land Rover would be useful later tonight. I didn't want to take a cab to Highgate Cemetery, loaded down with stakes and magical artifacts. It might just raise suspicion.

The busy streets meant that my journey to the museum was a long one and I sat in the back of the cab, learning the magical formula so that by the time I was dropped off outside the museum, I knew the sound combination without having to refer to the slip of paper.

It was still raining when I got out of the cab. I rushed across the forecourt between huddles of tourists in plastic ponchos toward the museum entrance, an imposing example of Greek revival architecture with high columns fashioned after the style of ancient Greek temples. When I got inside, out of the rain, I went to the ticket desk and bought a ticket to the Sunken Cities exhibition.

The museum was busy, buzzing with life and sound as visitors marveled at the high glass ceiling of the Great Court, the main entrance area of the museum. I'd been here before many times yet the grandeur of the building never failed to awe me. Unlike the tourists talking excitedly to each other, I had no one to speak to, and I felt alone in the vast architectural space. I wished Felicity could be here.

I was confident that I could tap into the statue's magic and open the locked door in my mind, but I had no idea what effect that would have on me. Would my memories return slowly in fragments or would they come flooding into my head like an unstoppable tidal wave? Tapping into powerful magic could be dangerous and I'd rather not do it alone.

But I had no choice. I strode purposefully across the Great Court to the Sunken Cities entrance and showed my ticket to the attendant there. Once inside, I pushed my way through the crowd in search of the statue of Hapi, God of the Nile Flood.

It wasn't too difficult to find a eighteen-foot-tall statue and when I reached it, I stood admiring it for a moment. This magical artifact had been buried in the silt at the bottom of the Nile for over a thousand years, and now I stood before it as the ancient Egyptians had once done when it stood in the temple at Heracleion.

The statue of Hapi had obviously been built to inspire awe, standing so high that my head was at the level of its knees. It depicted the god stepping forward with one great stone foot, holding a bowl in his arms, the bowl that symbolically contained the nourishment that the Nile floods brought to the land. Hapi wore a stone headdress that reached almost to the ceiling.

I tore my eyes away from the impressive piece of stonework and looked at the crowd around me. Dozens of people stood staring at the statue, some taking photos of it on their phones. I was obviously not going to get a quiet moment alone with the artifact. I was just going to have to go up to it and perform the ancient while tourists from all over the world watched me. Hopefully there wouldn't be any pyrotechnics or glowing sparks of magic because that would be tough to explain.

Taking a deep breath, I prepared myself to step up to the statue and lay my hands on it. Hopefully, I could speak the magical formula before I got thrown out by a security guard.

As I made my move, I felt a hand grab my arm and a woman's voice said, "Wait." This was ridiculous; I'd barely moved an inch before I'd been stopped. I turned around expecting to see one of the museum's guards.

Instead, I looked into the dark brown eyes of a woman I'd met once before. It took a moment for my brain to attach a name to the pretty Japanese woman who had grabbed me.

Then it came to me. I was standing face to face with Sumiko.

The *satori* who had stolen my memories.

CHAPTER 12

"WHAT THE HELL ARE YOU doing here?" I asked. "How did you find me?"

"I knew that you would be at this place at this moment. I also know why you are here."

"Yeah, to get back the memories you stole from me."

She shook her head. "No. Please, come with me and I will explain it to you." Stepping away from the statue she gestured for me to follow her.

I hesitated. This was the woman who had caused me so much trouble in Paris and then thrown a memory wipe into my head. Why should I trust her, or even listen to her? But looking at her pleading expression made me decide to follow her. Hell, she owed me an explanation, and the statue wasn't going anywhere.

She led me out of the Sunken Cities exhibition and back to the Great Court. I followed her to an area where the tourist traffic was relatively light. We could hear each other talk here but not be overheard because of the general background hum of voices.

"I came here to warn you," Sumiko said. "You helped me in Paris, so I feel I should repay the favor."

"You've already helped me more than enough. Your version of helping someone is to make them forget everything."

"No, you are wrong, Alec Harbinger. I am not guilty of what you are accusing me of."

"Then why can't I remember clearly what happened in Paris? Why can't I remember mailing an ancient Egyptian box to myself? And why did a witch tell me there's a magical locked door in my head?"

She nodded. "I altered your memory of Paris. I admit that. But I did so for your own good. I was trying to keep you out of trouble because you had been kind to me."

"Trouble is my business," I said. "I don't need you to decide what I can or can't remember about the events in my own life."

She lowered her eyes. "I thought I was doing you a kindness. I see now that I may have been wrong in that regard." She looked genuinely upset.

"Look," I said gently, "I know that you probably thought you were doing the right thing, but it isn't right to go messing with people's heads like that."

"Even if I did it to protect you?"

I frowned in confusion. "What do you mean?"

"What you remember of the events in Paris is a memory that I placed in your mind to protect not only you but the entire world. Your recollection is that after you found Pierre Louvain's body in his apartment, you went to the catacombs and fought some vampires before finding me with my dead captors. You then believe that you told me to flee the country because the Society of Shadows wanted me to join them, but you knew there were unknown members of the Society who could not be trusted. You did not want my power to fall into the wrong hands."

I nodded. "Yeah, that's exactly what I remember."

"None of these things are true."

"Oh, great. So where does reality end and the false memory begin?"

"After you found Pierre Louvain's body. You did not go to the catacombs and you did not fight vampires there. When I created the false memory, it had to be something that you would believe, that was consistent with your character, otherwise your mind would reject it eventually. Rescuing me from vampires was entirely consistent with who you are, so your mind readily accepted that memory as real."

"I didn't go to the catacombs that night?" My head was beginning to hurt.

"No, you did not."

"But Pierre Louvain left a message for my father. *L'empire de la mort.* Empire of the dead. I connected it to the inscription over the entrance to the catacombs. You may have wiped my memory, but my father got that message from Pierre."

"That was a coincidence that worked in my favor. Your father did receive the message and he told you about it. I made it seem to you that it referred to the Paris catacombs. That fitted neatly into the false memory. But Pierre was not speaking of the catacombs at all. He was referring to an actual empire of the dead. A world ruled by an army of the dead."

I was beginning to understand. "So the message gave you the idea for the catacomb story." When Devon Blackwell had touched me in the bookshop and whispered, "Empire of the dead," I'd thought she meant the catacombs. I had no ideas it was something much worse.

"So Pierre was referring to the Staff and Box of Midnight?" I asked Sumiko.

"Yes. He was not giving a location in that message, he was giving a warning."

I went over it in my mind, trying to take it all in. I'd always known my memory of Paris was false, but to learn that I hadn't gone to the catacombs that night and rescued Sumiko from vampires and rogue investigators was confusing.

"So what really happened that night?"

"I owe you an answer to that question," she said. "I was kidnapped, just as Pierre had reported. I allowed myself to be taken because I wished to learn who the kidnappers were and whether or not they knew the location of the Box of Midnight. My reason for being in Paris was to recover the Box of Midnight and take it somewhere safe where it could not be used by anyone."

"But it ended up in my possession," I said. "How did that happen?" I held up my hand. "Before you answer that, why not just give me my memory back now, since you're telling me what really happened anyway? You can return the memories to me, right?"

Sumiko nodded. "Yes, I could return the memories to you. But if I did so, it would endanger everything and everyone in this realm of existence."

I sighed. She was every bit as cryptic as the Coven. Why couldn't anyone speak plainly? "Endanger everyone in what way?" I asked, prompting her to explain further.

"While you were in Paris, you examined Pierre Louvain's notes and discovered that he had been working on a personal investigation during his free time, trying to find the exact location of a powerful relic. It was his hobby, a private obsession. When you saw his notes on the subject, you realized that he had solved the clues to the relic's whereabouts. But he knew that the relic was protected by a powerful guardian so he had not attempted to recover it. Also, the relic was so powerful that recovering it from its hiding place could mean the destruction of the world as we know it. After reading the notes, you asked me to erase the memory of the relic's location from your mind."

"I asked you to do this to me?"

Sumiko nodded. "And we destroyed the notebooks."

I guessed it made sense. If I knew where something so powerful was hidden, there was a risk of that information falling into the hands of bad people. The Midnight Cabal might be able to extract the information from me magically, and even the Society I worked for was compromised and couldn't be trusted. Luckily, Pierre had been killed because he had uncovered corruption within the Society, not because he was seeking an ultra-powerful artifact. His killers probably hadn't even bothered examining his notebooks.

Asking Sumiko to erase the location of such a powerful artifact from my head sounded like something I would do. So that explained why she was telling me about the events in Paris, but not restoring my memory. If I got all of my memories back, I'd be the possessor of some extremely dangerous information.

"Do you know where the relic is located?" I asked her.

"No, you did not tell me that information and I did not seek it in your mind when I took away your memory."

I ran over everything she had told me again. "Okay, so how did I get the Box of Midnight? How did I know to mail it to myself at Dearmont?"

"I told you to send it to yourself there. I have precognitive abilities. The future is not carved in stone and I see only possible outcomes, but the box must be in your possession for the most favorable outcomes to occur. There is a great evil roaming this world and for it to be destroyed, the Box of Midnight must be in Dearmont."

I ran a hand through my hair and watched a crowd of people going into the Sunken Cities exhibit. "So you knew why I was here today and you came to so stop me because I'd regain a memory of where a deadly artifact is hidden?"

She nodded.

"So I'm supposed to just walk out of here and live with a magical locked door in my head forever?" I wasn't sure I could do that, even if it was to protect some deadly secret. I may have asked Sumiko to erase the memory in the first place, but that was when I thought I'd be unaware of the memory wipe. Now that I knew about it, I couldn't stop thinking about it. It was like a broken tooth that you have to keep poking at with your tongue.

"The locked door in your mind was not my doing, Alec Harbinger."

"What do you mean it wasn't your doing? Of course it was. It's where you locked away the memories of what really happened in Paris, the location of the powerful relic."

She shook her head emphatically. "No. When I entered your mind to take away the memory of the relic, the locked door was already there."

I felt unstable suddenly, as if the floor of the museum might crack open at any time, plummeting me into a deep, dark hole. I felt cold, clammy. I leaned heavily against the wall.

Sumiko put her hands on my shoulders. "Alec Harbinger, are you all right?"

I breathed deeply in an attempt to clear my head, which felt as if someone had poured concrete into it through my ears. What did she mean the door was already there? How could that be possible? "I don't understand," I said.

She looked into my eyes earnestly. "When I met you in Paris, part of your memory was already locked behind a magical door."

CHAPTER 13

I HAVE TO TOUCH THE statue," I told Sumiko. "I don't have a choice now." The shock of learning that my mind had already been tampered with before Paris was slowly fading. I was considering my options in a detached, calm manner. At least, I thought I was, and the only solution I could see was to touch the statue of Hapi, recite the magical formula, and break down the door in my mind.

"But then you will learn the location of the relic," she said. "You asked me to remove that memory. The magical process you wish to undertake will reverse my work."

"If I don't do this, I'll never know what has been taken from me and locked away."

"Perhaps it has been locked away for good reason," she said.

"I won't know until I open the door."

She nodded slowly, looking crestfallen.

"Maybe after I've touched the statue, you can take away the memory of the relic's location again," I said.

"No. Altering someone's mind too many times is dangerous. You have had your memories altered by me and by someone before me. A third time could result in permanent damage."

"Then the location of the relic is a secret I'm going to have to live with and protect. Did I tell you what the relic is?"

"No, you did not." She looked over at the entrance to the Sunken Cities exhibit with a fearful gaze. "I have a bad feeling about this, Alec Harbinger."

"Can't your precognitive powers tell you what's going to happen if I go through with this?"

"I do not see everything in the future, only certain events. And even the things I do see can be changed. I do not know what will happen if you perform the magical process."

I hesitated, but only for a moment. I had to know what memory had been taken from me. Unfortunately, the location of an Armageddon-type relic came with that knowledge as a package deal, but there was nothing I could do about that. I strode back toward the Sunken Cities exhibit, my mind made up, my intention clear.

Sumiko remained in the Great Court, understanding that I had come to an irreversible decision and not trying to stop me.

When I got to the statue, I didn't let myself think about what I was about to do. I couldn't hesitate and risk talking myself out of this. I placed my hands on the statue's legs and closed my eyes, quietly reciting the magical formula that Felicity had researched.

The ancient stone was cold beneath my palms, but as I murmured the sounds that each hieroglyph in the formula represented, it seemed as if the statue grew warmer. As I continued, I felt a spark of energy jump between hands and the statue as if the stone were electrified and grounding its energy through my body.

The formula was short and I recited it quickly. As I sounded out the final syllable, I saw a white flash behind my eyelids and felt a searing heat in my head that lasted for a fraction of a second. The stone returned to being cold beneath my touch.

I opened my eyes and faced a crowd of onlookers who looked confused, bemused, and curious. Some of them took photos of me on their phones. I stepped away from the statue and walked slowly back out to the Great Court, searching my memory for anything new.

There was nothing.

Okay, so maybe the spell took some time to work. I could ask Sumiko to look into my mind and tell me if the magical door was still there. That way, I'd know if the formula had worked or if being buried in the silt at the bottom of the Nile for a thousand years had wrecked the statue's mojo.

But Sumiko was gone. I returned to the exact place I'd last seen her and scanned the faces around the Great Court. She was nowhere to be seen. The museum was busy but not so crowded that I would lose Sumiko in a sea of people. She'd left the building, taking with her the only chance I had at discovering if my encounter with Hapi had worked or not.

The flash of heat in my head suggested that something had happened, but it could all be nothing more than smoke and mirrors. I didn't want pyrotechnics, I wanted results.

Heading out the main door and into the rain, I decided to go back to the hotel and change into some dry clothes before calling the hospital to find out if Felicity had woken up.

As I walked through the museum's gates and onto the sidewalk, I smelled something that made me grimace. I was sure it was the ripe, rotten meat odor of a dead body.

I looked around. I couldn't see the source of the foul smell.

Spotting a black cab on the road, I waved at it and the driver pulled over. As I got in the back, I said, "You smell that? Smells like a dead dog or something."

He turned and frowned at me through the Plexiglas screen separating him from the passenger area. "No, mate, I can't smell anything. Where to?"

I gave him the name of my hotel and sat back, the stench of death still strong in the air.

Then a memory flashed into my head. I was standing near the dead body of Pierre Louvain, reading his notebooks. Sumiko was standing on the other side of the room, placing the Box of Midnight into a cardboard box. I could remember the notes written on the pages of the notebooks, in a code that was common among Society investigators but made all the more difficult to decipher because it translated into French and my knowledge of the language was rusty.

And, when he'd realized he was getting closer to finding the relic he sought, he'd changed the code in the book to a more obscure version that would be difficult to unlock for anyone not familiar with it. But to someone who had been sent to the Academy of Shadows at the age of ten and been curious enough to read some of the most obscure books in the Academy library, breaking the code was child's play.

As I read the code and translated it into French and then into English in my head, I realized the gravity of Pierre's discovery. I knew what the relic was and I knew where it was hidden.

As the memory faded, so did the smell of death that had seemed to fill the taxi. My brain had triggered the memory by first accessing my olfactory senses and then leading me into the scene. Was that how all the memories would begin, with a smell?

I looked out at London through the rain-streaked windows. The statue's spell seemed to be working slowly, bringing back memories of Paris in fractured pieces that would eventually fit together to form a whole. Hopefully, the memories that had been mysteriously locked behind a door in my mind would also return. Those memories were older than the Paris ones, so maybe they would take longer to return.

I had no idea. Magic wasn't an exact science.

But there was one thing I now knew, and with Pierre Louvain's death, I might be the only living person who knew it. It was something I had to keep secret. I couldn't even let anyone know that I knew such a secret.

As we drove through the cold, wet streets of London, I mentally told myself what I had discovered in Pierre's notes, the notes that had been destroyed for bearing such deadly knowledge: I knew the location of the Spear of Destiny, a spear that had been thrust through the side of Jesus while he was being crucified. The Spear was hidden in France, in the Abbey of Fontenay.

And although the Spear had been sought throughout history, most notably by Hitler and the Nazis, it must never be removed from its hiding place because it held a terrible power that could destroy the world. Pierre's notes had only hinted at the Spear's power but I'd heard in the past that the two-thousand-year-old weapon could tear the barriers between realms. With such a weapon, the Midnight Cabal could destroy the world. I shivered slightly and asked the cab driver to turn up the heat in the car.

He obliged and caught my eyes in the rear view mirror. "You all right back there?" he asked. "You look like you've seen a ghost."

CHAPTER 14

BY EARLY AFTERNOON, I WAS riding the elevator up to the ward where Felicity was being cared for. After I'd returned to the hotel from the museum, I'd called the hospital and been told by a nurse that Felicity was awake and I could visit her after lunch. I'd gotten into the Land Rover and driven over here immediately.

When the elevator doors opened, I hoped that Jason wasn't here. I couldn't be held responsible for my actions if he was.

But there was nobody in her room except Felicity and a nurse who was fussing over the machines by the bed.

Felicity's face lit up when she saw me. "Alec!" She sat up in bed and put out her arms for a hug.

I held her for a moment and murmured, "I'm so glad you're okay." It felt good to be close to her, to feel her head nestled against my shoulder.

"I'm fine," she said when I released her and pulled up a chair to her bedside. "The doctors say I should be out of here tomorrow."

"That's great. And you put the flowers I brought into a vase." I pointed at the bouquet of hyacinths and daffodils that had been placed into a glass vase near the sink.

"Oh. Did you send those? I didn't know who they were from. A nurse put them in water for me. Thank you."

"I was here yesterday," I said. "You wouldn't remember, though, because you were Sleeping Beauty in the bed. Didn't Jason tell you I'd been here?"

She shook her head. "No. Maybe he forgot. He's been out of his mind with worry."

"Yeah," I said flatly.

"So, how are you?" Felicity asked. "For someone who just survived a plane crash, you look very well."

"I'm fine. The pilot did a great job of landing on the water. After that, it was a long wait for the Society to pick us up from a nearby aircraft carrier. Boring, really."

She laughed. It was good to hear. "Only Alec Harbinger would call being attacked by demons and crash-landing in the sea boring."

The nurse finished whatever she was doing with the machines and told Felicity she would be back later. She gave me a smile and left the room.

"I went to the museum today," I told Felicity when we were alone.

Excitement flashed in her dark eyes. "Did you see the statue? What happened?"

"I did the ritual and it worked. At least I think it did. I can remember more about Paris now, anyway."

"That's great. So what really happened there?"

"There'll be plenty of time to talk about that when you're better. I met the *satori* at the museum, too."

"The *satori* from Paris? What was she doing there?"

"Mostly talking in riddles. She explained that I sent the Box of Midnight to myself because she told me to. Apparently, there's something evil roaming the earth and the box has to be in Dearmont for the evil to be eventually destroyed."

Felicity frowned. "What is that supposed to mean?"

"Your guess is as good as mine. I've heard enough enigmatic prophecies to last a lifetime. There's something else too: the magical door in my mind that Devon Blackwell saw wasn't put there by the *satori*. It was already there when I went to Paris. Whatever memories are behind that door were locked away by someone else."

Her eyes went wide. "What? How did that happen? When?"

I shrugged. "I have no idea. Hopefully, I'll have more of a clue when the memories return. The statue ritual worked in regard to the Paris memories—they're slowly coming back to me—so I'm hoping it also unlocked the door in my head. There's no way of knowing until I remember something that was once hidden from me."

"Oh my God, Alec, that's terrible."

"Yeah, well, it's just something I have to live with for now. I'm sure it'll all get resolved eventually. But I'm not here to talk about my problems. How are you feeling? Are they looking after you?"

"Yes, everyone here is great. All of the doctors and nurses looking after me are working for the Society, so I don't have to be careful about what I say. They know all about demon poison and things like that." Her face grew concerned and she asked, "Who do you think sent those demons to attack us?"

"My dad thinks it's an evil secret society. I'm not so sure. That big red demon knew my name, so it reminded me of the ogres and Tunnock being sent to kill me. Or maybe my dad's right and those in the evil secret society know me by name, but I find that hard to believe. I'm nobody special, just an investigator."

"Do you think it's connected to the Box of Midnight?"

"It could be. Tunnock said that his employer wanted me dead so that I couldn't use the box against him. Maybe his employer is this evil being that's roaming the earth and has heard the same prophecy the *satori* told me, that the box being in Dearmont will mean his eventual destruction. So he hired some supernatural goons to take me out and prove the prophecy wrong."

She nodded and said, "That box may have a curse attached to its destruction, but it seems to be a curse just to have it in your possession."

"Yeah, you got that right. I feel bad leaving Mallory babysitting the damn thing."

She looked at me and I saw tears in her eyes. "Maybe you should go back to Dearmont to make sure she's okay."

"Yeah, just as soon as they let you leave this place."

Felicity shook her head slowly. "No, Alec. You should go. Leave me here." A tear ran down her right cheek and she wiped it away with the sleeve of her hospital gown.

"I'm not leaving you," I said softly.

"You have to." There was a note of despair in her voice. "I'm not coming back to Dearmont, Alec. You'll have to give my job to someone else."

I felt a hollowness in the pit of my stomach. "There isn't anyone else who can do it. You're my assistant, Felicity. What about your dream of being an investigator?" I realized that my voice sounded as if I was pleading with her, but I didn't care. I couldn't sit here and let her throw away her life, her dream. "It's what you always wanted."

"I was wrong," she said simply. "I can't live my life looking over my shoulder, waiting to be attacked by some monster from Hell. I'm not that kind of person."

"You're exactly that kind of person. You're tough, resilient. You saved my life."

"And look what happened to me. I ended up in here. What if that demon poison had been fatal?"

"It wasn't."

"This time. What about next time, or the time after that? I can't risk being killed because I'm not investigator material. There are people who love me and it would destroy them if I were gone."

"You mean Jason," I said.

"And my parents. And what about you? Wouldn't you be upset if I was killed?"

"Of course I would. I'd be devastated. But there are more ways to die than fighting monsters."

She narrowed her dark eyes. "What is that supposed to mean?"

"I mean settling with Jason and trying to live a mundane life. That isn't you, Felicity."

"Do you mean settling *with* Jason, or settling *for* Jason?" She was angry now.

"I mean both," I said truthfully. No one could say I didn't know how to make a bad situation worse.

"Oh, right. Just because he isn't a good-looking preternatural investigator who spends his life fighting evil, you think he's nothing."

"I didn't say that. I just don't think he's the right guy for you. You have a sense of adventure, a daring personality. And you have a talent that would be wasted if you lived a normal life. You're nothing like Jason. Do you think he would have attacked that demon on the plane? Or would he be cowering in a corner somewhere while it choked the life out of me?"

She hesitated. We both knew the answer to that question, but Felicity wasn't going to admit it. "You don't know what he'd do, you don't know him. And as for living a normal life, not everyone wants to spend their life dealing with demons, werewolves, and changelings. Some people just want a normal life. That isn't a bad thing."

"I know that, but it isn't...."

"Just go, Alec." She turned away from me and folded her arms. The tears flowed freely now and she didn't bother to wipe them away.

"If you like, I'll come back tomorrow and we can...."

"Please go." She didn't look at me. Her teary eyes were fixed on the foot of the bed.

I sighed and stood up. There didn't seem to be anything I could say that would change her mind. "Can I come and see you tomorrow?"

"No, Alec. You'll only try to convince me to go back to Dearmont with you and I can't. I just can't."

"We don't have to talk about Dearmont. We can talk about anything you want."

She began to cry harder. "Please leave."

I couldn't bear to think that this was the end of the road for Felicity and me but I respected her wishes and left the room, feeling the hollowness in my gut become a black hole that felt like it would swallow me up entirely.

I got to the elevator and hit the button, wondering why I could smell gasoline. I looked around the ward for the source of the smell but couldn't see anything that would give off such a strong odor.

When I got into the elevator and jabbed the button to take me down to the first floor—which was marked with a "G" because the British called the floor at street level the ground floor.

The smell of gas was getting stronger.

An image flashed into my mind. I was in a car, in the back seat. My mother was in the driver's seat. Something was wrong. The windshield was obscured by a spider web of cracks shooting through the glass. The smell of gas filled the air and I could see white smoke rising beyond the side windows.

My mom turned in her seat, her face full of concern. "Alec, are you okay?"

"Yeah, I think so," I said. My voice sounded young, high-pitched.

"Listen closely," she said. "You need to get out of the car and run. You see those woods over there?"

I looked out of my window. All I could see was smoke and beyond that, the darkness of the night. But I didn't want to disappoint my mom, so I said, "Yeah, I see them."

"I want you to go ahead and open your door and run into the woods, okay?" She cast a nervous glance at the rearview mirror.

I could hear footsteps behind the car. They approached slowly, carefully.

"Alec, go," my mom said. "And whatever happens, don't look back, okay?"

"But, Mom...."

"Please, Alec. Run for the trees. And don't stop running."

Confused and scared, but determined to do what my mom asked, I unfastened my seatbelt and opened the car door. The smell of gas and burning rubber made the night air acrid. My eyes began to water.

My mom's eyes were watering too, or maybe she was crying, when she reached out to touch my arm and said, "I love you, Alec. No matter what happens in your life, always remember that I loved you."

I hesitated, unsure what to say.

"Now go," she whispered. "Hurry." I slid out of the car and, just as I had been told by my mom, I ran for the trees which I could now see at the side of the road. The night was cold but hot tears streamed down my cheeks as I ran for the cover of darkness.

Despite being told to not look back, my childlike curiosity got the better of me and I glanced over my shoulder to see if my mother was following me. She wasn't. I saw four dark figures walking calmly up to the burning, crumpled car. Then a flash of intense blue light shot from the vehicle and one of the figures fell to the ground. The other three hesitated for a moment before rushing the car.

"Run, Alec!" my mother shouted.

I ran. Behind me, flashes of light of various colors illuminated the sky as if someone were igniting fireworks.

I ran through the night, branches and pine needles whipping at my face and arms, the sharp pain nothing compared to the crushing sorrow I felt inside. Tears streamed from my eyes and I kept repeating to myself that my mom was gone. I would never see her again. They had killed her.

The memory receded and the elevator door opened with a ding. I stepped out, realizing that I'd been crying, wiping the tears away with my sleeve. I had always believed that when my mom had been killed in a car crash, I'd been at my aunt's house. I had a memory of an Oregon police officer coming to the house and telling my aunt that her sister had been killed on the highway.

But when I tried to recall details of that memory now, I couldn't. It was being replaced with the memory of what really happened that night. My mother had been murdered. And I'd been in the car with her moments before.

Knowing the truth made me feel the loss of my mom all over again. I left the hospital and walked through the afternoon rain with a heavy heart. When I got into the Land Rover, I rested my head on the steering wheel and let the tears flow.

The words that my ten-year-old self kept repeating ran through my mind over and over. *She's gone. I'll never see her again.*

I wasn't sure how long I sat in the hospital parking lot like that but when I was done and I had no more tears left, the sorrow that had overwhelmed me turned to rage. My mother had been murdered and I'd been in the car with her moments before. Someone had taken my memory of that night and locked it away in my mind.

They'd stolen the truth from me.

As I started the engine, I glanced at the hospital entrance and saw Jason Farmer, carrying a huge bouquet of flowers tied with a pink ribbon, heading inside. He'd gotten what he wanted. It seemed like the life he had planned for himself and Felicity was going to happen after all. And, knowing Felicity's personality, I was sure that life wasn't going to be kind to her.

I also understood the awful loss it meant for the Society, the world, and me.

I let out a slow breath and resisted the urge to corner Jason in the elevator and beat the shit out of him.

Instead, I drove out of the parking lot and onto the busy streets of London. The day was drawing to a close and I couldn't say I was sorry to see it go. In a few hours, the night would fall and then I would be able to release the anger I felt building inside me.

Soon, it would be time to kill some vampires.

CHAPTER 15

MY FATHER CALLED ME AT eleven and asked me to meet him in the hotel's underground parking garage. I rode the elevator down, feeling anxious and fully alert. I'd spent the evening in my room, replaying the memory of my mother's death over and over, trying to remember some detail that would give me a clue to her killers' identities. I'd come up with nothing, so, after a meal of chicken and pasta in the hotel's restaurant, I'd sat on the bed and watched TV. Eventually, I'd fallen asleep. Now, I was fully awake and full of nervous energy.

I got out of the elevator to find a black Bentley parked next to the Land Rover. As I approached, a driver, neatly dressed in a dark uniform and cap, got out of the Bentley and opened the rear door. My father got out.

He was dressed in a tweed jacket, green trousers and high boots. On his head, he wore a deerstalker hat, the kind that was worn by Sherlock Holmes. In fact, my father looked like he had stepped from the pages of a 1920s adventure novel and was ready to go plundering tombs in Egypt or search for lost treasure in the jungle.

"Ready for some vampire hunting, my lad?" he asked when he saw me.

"Ready as I'll ever be."

"Good. Get the Land Rover open and we'll put the weapons inside." He motioned to the driver who opened the Bentley's trunk and took out a long, black canvas bag.

I opened the back of the Land Rover and the bag was placed inside.

"That will be all," my dad told the driver. The driver nodded and got back into the Bentley. A few seconds later, he was driving away, leaving us with the smell of exhaust fumes. The smell reminded me of the crashed car I'd been inside with my mom during her final moments of life.

Shaking the thought away, I pointed at the canvas bag. "What have we got?"

He grinned and opened the bag. Reaching inside, he took out a pistol crossbow and handed it to me. "We've got these beauties. And plenty of wood-tipped bolts. Perfect for vampire slaying."

I inspected the pistol crossbow. It was a weapon I was familiar with, a self-cocking version that meant it could be reloaded quickly by pulling on a lever behind the handle.

These would be useful against the vampires at the cemetery. That was, of course, assuming there were actual vampires there. We were only going on the prophecy of the Coven and that hadn't exactly been clear in its meaning.

"Regular stakes," my dad said, removing a half dozen carved lengths of wood from the bag and laying them next to each other in a neat line. "And to capture John DuMont, I have these." He showed me a set of heavy iron shackles. I could see magical symbols carved into the metal cuffs and the chain. "Enchanted, of course. Once we get these on him, he won't escape."

"And how are we supposed to get them on him in the first place?" I asked.

"I admit, it will be tricky," he said. "The Coven has informed me that DuMont may have aligned himself with a demon. That's why I brought these." He removed two sheathed swords from the bag and placed them next to the stakes. Like the shackles, the sword hilts were inscribed with magical symbols.

"A demon, huh? Do those witches know everything?"

"They seem able to find out most things," he said. "But as you know, their method of relaying the information isn't always concise. Some days are more informative than others when dealing with the Coven."

"Did you ever ask them about mom's death?"

He looked at me, shocked. "What? Why would I ask that? Your mother was killed in a car accident."

"Was she? How can we be sure?"

My dad frowned. "Alec, the Oregon police found her body in her car by the side of the road. She crashed and didn't get out in time before flames engulfed the car."

I studied his face as he spoke. He seemed upset. So maybe he'd been told the same story I had and believed it without question. I felt guilty for suspecting that my own father might know more about my mom's death than he'd told me, or even that he could be involved in removing my memory of that night on the highway, but I had to check.

"She was the wife of a high level Society member, Dad. Maybe she was killed because of that."

A sadness crept into his eyes. "Alec, when your mother took you to America, she severed all ties with me and the Society. She didn't want you to be involved in ... all this." He indicated to the weapons in the back of the Land Rover. "I respected her wishes and let her raise you however she saw fit. There was no foul play regarding her death. It's just one of those unfortunate things that happen in life sometimes. It's nobody's fault. I know you want there to be a bad guy somewhere so you can hunt him down, but in this case, you just have to accept what happened."

I shrugged and closed the trunk before getting into the driver's seat. My dad obviously didn't know that there was a bad guy somewhere. And I *was* going to hunt him down. Hunt him down and kill him for what he did to my mother.

Dad climbed into the passenger seat and looked at me closely. "Are you all right? You seem distracted tonight."

"Yeah," I said, starting the engine and backing out of the parking space. "I'm worried about having to protect your ass from vampires."

"Well, there's really no need. I was doing this kind of thing before you were born."

"That's what I mean, Dad. That was a long time ago."

He went quiet until we were on the street. Then, he said, "What we're doing tonight is very important, Alec. If we can capture DuMont and get him back to headquarters for questioning, we might be able to flush out all of the traitors in the organization. I've dedicated my life to the Society of Shadows, and I'll do anything to help get rid of those who would betray its values. I won't see it destroyed from within by people like DuMont." He spat out the name as if it pained him to speak it.

"Okay, Dad, but if things get too dangerous and I tell you to get back to the Land Rover, you do it. You have to agree to that or I'm going to turn around right now and spend the rest of the night watching TV in my hotel room."

He sighed in frustration. "Yes, I agree. Although I don't know why I'm letting you dictate terms to me. I'm the superior officer on this mission."

"And I'm a concerned son who doesn't want to see his dad get killed by a creature of the night."

"You know, it might be better if you had a little faith in your old man," he said.

I didn't say anything. I was worried about him being in the field and there was nothing he could say that would make me feel comfortable about going into a dangerous situation with him by my side.

We drove in silence for a while toward Highgate, a bright, waxing moon visible in the sky when the clouds weren't obscuring it. At least it had stopped raining.

As we reached Swain's Lane, where the cemetery was located, my father looked across at me with a wry smile. "Look at us, Alec. Father and son working together for the Society, ready to kill vampires and catch a villain. We make a good team, wouldn't you say?"

"Yeah, sure." I just hoped that both members of the team were going to go home alive tonight.

Highgate Cemetery was split into two section, the East and West. The older graves, including the Lebanon Circle, were located in the West Cemetery farther along the road on our left. On our right, beyond its low wall and iron railings, the East Cemetery was dark and quiet.

As we reached the tall building that marked the entrance to the West Cemetery, I parked the Land Rover and killed the engine.

The night was silent.

We got out and, without a word, went to the back of the Land Rover and distributed the weapons among ourselves. I fixed one of the sheathed swords to my belt, shoved a couple of stakes through my belt at the other hip, and placed the pistol crossbow bolts, which were in a small leather quiver, into my inside jacket pocket. I levered the loading mechanism on my crossbow and loaded a bolt but left the safety on for now.

While my dad armed himself in a similar manner, I picked up the heavy iron shackles and draped them around my neck. They were heavy and made moving more difficult, but at least they didn't clank together as they would if they were hanging off my belt.

Ghostly moonlight broke through the clouds. I didn't need my Maglite to see that the large iron gates beneath the building's archway were open. I pointed the open gates out to my dad.

He nodded grimly. "The game is afoot."

We made our way beneath the archway and peered through the open gates. The area beyond was an open space bordered by a long colonnade. To either side, paths led to the graves and mausoleums that had been here since Victorian times. There was a smell of wet grass and trees in the air from the earlier rainfall, but nothing seemed out of the ordinary.

I gestured for my dad to follow and crept along a path that I knew would lead us to the Egyptian Gate, a faux-ancient gate that led to Egyptian Avenue. Beyond the avenue, which was lined with tombs in the ancient Egyptian style, lay the Circle of Lebanon where the witches of the Coven had prophesied John DuMont would be tonight.

As we passed by various gravestones and mausoleums, I kept a tight grip on the pistol crossbow. If there were vampires here, they could be hiding anywhere.

"Stay close, Dad," I whispered.

"I will, Son." He was scanning the graves on his side of the path, occasionally turning to check behind us, both hands holding his pistol crossbow steady.

His earlier bravado had disappeared and he looked worried. I couldn't blame him. Hell, I was scared. Vampires weren't pushovers and who knew what powers John DuMont had, especially if he had sided with a demon?

We didn't even know why he was in the cemetery in the first place. Whatever his reason for being here, it wasn't to lay flowers on anyone's grave, that was for sure. Magic and death only ever mixed together in ways that could be described as evil or wicked.

We reached the Egyptian Gate, an archway in a high stone wall flanked by faux pillars. The iron gates in the archway were open, just like the ones at the cemetery's street entrance.

I stepped forward to pass through to Egyptian Avenue but stopped as the metallic smell of blood reached me. I wondered if I was actually smelling it or if my mind was fooling me again, recalling the tang of blood from one of my lost memories.

"Dad, do you smell that?"

He sniffed the air. "Blood."

It wasn't a buried memory resurfacing; it was here, now. A hissing sounded from the darkness and the first vampire dropped to the ground from where he must have been hiding in the roof of the archway. I heard a rustling behind us and turned to face two more vampires creeping out from behind a mausoleum.

My dad and I stood back to back, my pistol crossbow wavering between the two undead creatures coming from behind the mausoleum, his aimed at the one in the archway.

The three vampires rushed us and I shouted, "Fire!"

CHAPTER 16

I PULLED THE CROSSBOW TRIGGER and the wood-tipped bolt flew at the vampire closest to me. The bolt was fast but the undead creature was faster. He dodged the shot and the bolt shattered against the stone wall of the mausoleum.

Dropping the crossbow because there was no time to reload it, I reached my hands down to my hips in a cross draw motion, simultaneously unsheathing the sword with one hand and grabbing a stake with the other.

The vampire I hadn't shot at was almost on me and I extended the drawing motion of the sword to slice the blade up along his body when he jumped at me.

He screamed in agony and dark blood stained his sweater, but I knew the sword couldn't finish him like this. He would recover from such a cut in seconds. The only way to end him with the sword was to cut off his head. Still, the force of my attack kept him off me. He had meant to land on me and drive me to the ground, probably while ripping my throat out with his teeth, but I was spared that agonizing death for now.

While he writhed on the ground bleeding, his companion came in fast, his fangs bared. Either he'd been distracted by the bright blue glow of the enchanted sword or he simply hadn't noticed the stake in my other hand. When he came forward, I lunged like a fencer, driving the wood through his skin and into his chest.

His eyes went wide and he fell to the ground, his body decomposing so fast that by the time he landed on path, he was nothing more than a skeleton and a few scraps of rotted flesh.

The stench of the sudden decomposition hit me and I wanted to vomit, but I didn't have time for that. The vampire I'd cut with the sword was coming back for more.

I risked a quick glance at the archway where my dad was fighting in hand-to-hand combat with his vamp. I didn't give much for his chances. I needed to get rid of my guy and help my dad as soon as I could. That was assuming I could actually get rid of my guy.

He didn't leap at me, having learned his lesson from the last time he tried that move. Instead, he kept his distance, weighing me up, looking for a chance to get past my defenses. I held the sword in one hand, his blood still dripping from its blade, and the stake in the other, his companion's blood staining the wood. He knew I wasn't going to make it easy for him.

"Human," he said in a low tone, "I will drink of your blood until I am sated and then I shall leave your body for the crows."

"Give it your best shot," I said, looking him in the eye. I wasn't worried about his glamor ability because to do that, to take control of a human's mind, the vampire needed the mind in question to be in a receptive state. Facing him in a fight to the death hardly made me receptive to his commands.

My words angered him. He hissed and moved forward, trying to come under my weapons, probably hoping to use his fangs to rip into my torso.

As he lowered his body and rushed me, I sliced down with the sword. Its enchanted blade sliced into the vampire's shoulder and I put all of my weight behind the blow, forcing the creature to the ground. He lay on his stomach, fighting against the blade that pinned him, cursing me and clawing at the air.

I knelt down and drove the stake into his back. His cry pierced the night for a fraction of a second and then he was silent as the rapid decomposition process began. I got back to my feet and pulled the second stake from my belt, ready to help my father.

But when I looked over toward the archway, my dad was standing over a pile of rotted flesh and bones. The stake he had used to kill the vamp protruded from the gore at his feet, driven through the creature with such force that it stood upright in the dirt.

"I forgot how much these things stink," Dad said, wrinkling his nose.

A wave of relief washed over me. Then I felt guilty for feeling so relieved. Maybe I should have had more faith in the old man after all.

"You okay?" I asked him.

"Yes, Alec, stop fussing over me. Now, let's go." He pointed at the archway that led to Egyptian Avenue.

I wiped the blade of my sword on the wet grass and slid it back into the sheath, then put the stakes back into my belt. Picking up the pistol crossbow and reloading it, I said, "Okay, let's go."

We passed beneath the Egyptian Gate and discovered where the smell of blood was coming from. It looked like the vampires had brought along a midnight snack. Two dead bodies, a man and a woman, lay in the darkness. It looked like they'd been feasted on by the vamps until they'd died of blood loss.

"Horrible way to go," my father said as we stepped over the bodies.

The Egyptian Avenue, lined with tombs, stretched before us, leading to the Circle of Lebanon, a sunken ring of tombs built around an ancient cedar tree. Standing beneath the tree was a man dressed in a long black coat, white shirt with lace collar and cuffs that looked like they belonged in the early eighteenth century, and dark breeches over high black boots. His black hair was long and unruly, blowing in the night breeze. He was handsome and his features made him appear to be in his mid-thirties, but his dark eyes gave the impression of a man much older than the face suggested.

When he saw us, he smiled and gestured for us to come closer. The smile was lizard-like and I got the feeling we were like two bugs about to be eaten. There was a sense of power emanating from this man that made me want to run all the way back through the cemetery and drive away as fast as I could.

"Is that DuMont?" I whispered to my father.

"No," he said. "I don't know who he is."

"Forgive me," the man beneath the tree said, "I haven't introduced myself. My name is John Polidori. Perhaps you've heard of me. I know who you are, of course. Thomas and Alec Harbinger, members of the Society of Shadows. I apologize for the treatment you received at the hands of my lackeys. I asked them to bring you to me, but something obviously was misinterpreted somewhere along the way and they tried to kill you. Oh well, all's well that ends well, I suppose, and vampire lackeys are ten-a-penny these days, so I won't have any trouble replacing them."

Dad looked at me and raised his eyebrows questioningly. "Do you think that's really John Polidori?"

I shrugged. John Polidori had been Lord Byron's physician in the 1800s. He'd been at Byron's Lake Geneva chateau on the night Mary Shelley had written *Frankenstein*.

That same night, Polidori had written *The Vampyre*, the first vampire story in the English language.

I'd seen a few things in my life that most people would call impossible, so this man's claim—that he was a doctor and writer from the nineteenth century who had known Byron, Mary Shelley, and her husband, the poet Percy Shelley—wasn't something I'd dismiss out of hand. Of course, if he really was Polidori and was alive today, looking so young, he had to be a vampire himself.

"No need to look so confused," he said. "Yes, I'm a vampire. That little story I wrote was partly autobiographical." He grinned and extended his fangs.

I drew my sword. The enchanted glow lit up the tombs and the ancient tree with a bright blue light. I didn't care if this guy had been around for over two hundred years; if he thought he was going to take us on, he'd better have some kickass moves.

Polidori frowned at me. "There's no need for that, Alec. I'm not here to fight."

"Are you here to meet John DuMont?" I asked. "We were told he'd be here tonight."

"Yes, so was I. But I'm afraid he must have known we were coming. He isn't here." He stepped forward and floated toward us, landing gently just a few feet in front of us. Now that he was closer, I could see the pale hue of his skin in the blue glow from my sword. I still held the weapon in my hand and I wasn't ready to put it away just yet. If he really was over two hundred years old, he'd be much stronger than the vamps we'd dealt with at the Egyptian Gate.

So the witches had been wrong about John DuMont. They'd been right about the vampires, but had led us to believe the creatures were working for DuMont. Well, actually, the witches had been so vague that we had assumed the vamps were working for DuMont. Coming to Highgate Cemetery had been a waste of time; we were no closer to catching the traitor.

"Why are you interested in DuMont?" I asked Polidori. "Are you working for him?"

He laughed. "Working *for* him? I'm not even working *with* him. I came here to kill the bastard."

I wasn't sure I believed him, but I asked, "Why?"

"Because you two weren't going to do it. He's too powerful. So I came to lend a hand."

"You knew we were coming here?" my father asked.

"Of course, Thomas. Your Society isn't the only place one can find witches with the power of prophecy. DuMont was supposed to be here tonight to perform some sort of ritual. I was told that you and your son would arrive on the scene to capture him. I came to help you. Well, honestly, I came to kill him. He's too dangerous to be allowed to live."

"I don't get it," I told him. "What's your interest in this?"

He looked at me as if I had asked the stupidest question in the world. "You know what he's trying to do, don't you? He's in league with an ancient demon called Rekhmire who wants to raise an army of the dead. DuMont is trying to make that possible by finding an ancient box that powers a staff he has in his possession."

"The Staff of Midnight," I said.

Polidori nodded. "I've heard it called that, yes."

"Rekhmire was the High Priest of Heliopolis. He created the staff and the box that powers it by imprisoning a sorceress's heart inside the box. He tried to raise an army in ancient Egypt but was defeated by the pharaoh. Then Rekhmire disappeared."

"Well, he's a demon now," Polidori said simply. "And he's using DuMont to find the box so he can raise another army of the dead."

"We have to stop him," my dad said.

"Yeah," I said. I looked at Polidori. "But I still don't get why you're so interested in stopping DuMont. An army of the dead sounds like a vampire's wet dream to me."

"An army of zombies destroying the human race is not what any vampire wants," Polidori said. He looked genuinely offended that I could suggest such a thing. "We have co-existed with humans for millennia. Rekhmire's motives are apocalyptic. Tell me, Alec, how would you respond if someone threatened to destroy all the cattle on the earth?"

"So that's what humans are to you? Cattle?"

He sighed. "To the younger vampires, that is true enough. They see humans simply as a food source and nothing more. But to the older generation, like myself, and those I serve, who are much older than me, humans are much more than simply food. You are entertainment, friends, sometimes allies, sometimes enemies. The relationship between vampires and humans is much more than consumer and food. But, yes, if Rekhmire destroys all of humanity with his army of the dead, the vampires will eventually starve. We need your blood for our own existence to continue."

"All right, you've convinced me we're on the same side where Rekhmire is concerned." I sheathed my sword. "So what do we do now? How do we stop him?"

"We can't get to Rekhmire," he said. "He has DuMont doing all the dirty work for him. I wouldn't be surprised if Rekhmire is in a different realm of existence at the moment. But we can stop Rekhmire by thwarting DuMont. And we do that by using the box against him."

"Use the box against him?" I didn't tell him that I knew where the box was. I didn't trust him that much.

Polidori grinned at me, a flicker of amusement in his dark eyes. "Alec, I know you must have the box. I was told by a witch that you are destined to destroy the heart inside it. Rekhmire and DuMont have obviously heard the same thing, which is why they've been trying to kill you."

My father looked at me with a shocked expression. "Alec, is this true? You have the box that DuMont wants?"

I gave Polidori a dirty look and sighed. "Yes, Dad, I have the box."

His brows knitted together angrily. "And when were you going to tell me that snippet of information?"

I shrugged. "I didn't know it was DuMont who wanted it." I looked at Polidori. "Are you sure that's what I'm supposed to do? Destroy it?" I had no intention of destroying the damned heart inside the box; I didn't want to be cursed by the "one year to live" thing.

"That's the prophecy," Polidori said. "But that doesn't mean it's necessarily going to happen. These things are much more fluid than that. Otherwise, I would have simply stayed out of the way and let you do what you are prophesied to do. But here I am, trying to kill DuMont myself. I don't trust prophecy, Alec."

"Neither do I," I said. "And I have no intention of destroying the Box of Midnight."

Polidori said, "Hmm, I know why." He nodded almost imperceptibly toward my father and raised his eyebrows questioningly. I shook my head. My dad knew nothing of the curse attached to the box and I wanted to keep it that way. Polidori nodded at me, telling me he would keep quiet about it. I hoped I could trust him on that.

My dad was no fool, though. He noticed the non-verbal exchange between Polidori and me. "What do you mean? Why won't you destroy it?"

I fielded his question casually but I doubted I was fooling anyone. "You know what it's like destroying magical artifacts, Dad. Most of them can only be destroyed by certain methods and then you have to deal with the sudden release of magical energy. It's a pain in the ass."

"But worth it if it means we can stop a madman from causing an apocalypse," he said.

He was right. Maybe it was worth it. If I destroyed the box, I would only have a year left to live, but wasn't that a small price to pay for saving the world? If DuMont got his way and raised an army of the dead for Rekhmire, we'd all end up dead anyway.

"If we don't destroy it," Dad continued, "perhaps we can hide it somewhere DuMont won't find it. The Society has a number of vaults that are hidden and well-guarded."

"It doesn't matter where we hide the box; DuMont can find it as long as he has the staff. The two items are connected to each other."

"DuMont has great magical power," Polidori said, "given to him by his infernal master. No matter how well-guarded your vaults, I fear DuMont would break through your defenses."

"You have to destroy the box, Alec," Dad said. He had no idea what he was saying, what the consequences were.

"Yes, you do," Polidori agreed. He knew exactly what he was telling me to do and he seemed amused by it.

I shrugged and said, "Sure." I had to get back to Maine anyway. DuMont was bound to show up there sooner or later once the staff led him to the box. I might be able to come up with a different plan in the meantime, one that didn't involve me getting cursed with a death sentence.

"I'll fly back home tomorrow," I told my dad. "And do what has to be done."

"I'll come with you."

"You need to be here, Dad, to root out the other traitors in the Society. I can handle this one on my own. Besides, there are a few people in Dearmont who will help me."

Polidori nodded to me. "I'll see you in Dearmont, Alec."

"There's no need for you to…."

"Still, I'd like to make sure that you do what you are destined to do." He grinned knowingly at me.

He wanted to make sure I went through with it. What was he going to do if I didn't? Force me to destroy the sorceress's heart?

"Fine," I said.

Polidori gave my father a nod and said, "Mr. Harbinger, it was a pleasure." With that, he turned and disappeared into the night.

"Well, this was an interesting evening," my dad said.

"Yeah, we should go hunting together more often," I said.

We walked back along the Egyptian Avenue and past the gate where we'd killed the vamps.

"Would you like to come back to the house for a drink?" Dad asked. "We could both use one after tonight. I've got some beer in especially for you."

"I'd love to, Dad, but I need to get back to the hotel and get some sleep. Can you arrange a plane to take me back home tomorrow?"

His face fell for just a moment but then he hid his disappointment. "Of course. I'll arrange a flight for you and Miss Lake first thing tomorrow morning."

"Felicity won't be going back with me," I said, feeling the loss of my assistant sharply as I spoke the words. "She's decided to stay here."

He looked surprised. "Oh, so you won't have an assistant. I'll see to it that you get someone new as soon as possible."

I stopped walking and spun him around to face me. "Why, Dad? Most investigators don't have assistants, so why is it so important to you that I have one?"

He shrugged, searching for an answer. "You're my son. I want to make sure you're okay."

"No, there's more to it than that. You sent Felicity to spy on me. I want to know why."

"You don't want another assistant," he said, ignoring me and setting off along the moonlit path again. "That's fine, Alec."

I caught up with him. We were almost at the main gate now and he was striding along as if he had to get through it as quickly as possible. He couldn't escape me that easily; we still had to drive back together.

"I just want to know why, Dad. I never had an assistant in Chicago, so why did you send Felicity to spy on me when I moved to Dearmont?"

"Because," he said, turning to face me angrily, "your mind had been played with by that damned *satori*. I wanted to know what damage she'd done, how you would be affected."

"All she did was remove a couple of days from my memory," I said. "It was no big deal. Certainly not a big enough deal to send someone to spy on me."

"Well, I thought it might be. Aren't I allowed to worry about my own son?" He turned on his heels and started for the gate again.

"You never worried about me before, so why start now?" I shouted after him.

He marched through the gate with no reply.

I followed him out to where I'd left the Land Rover. He was talking on his phone. After ending the call, he turned to me and said, "There's no need to give me a lift back. My driver is coming to pick me up." He folded his arms and stood staring at the road, his face stony.

"Look, Dad, there's no need to...."

"You go back to your hotel and get some rest. I'll text you the details of your flight."

There was no talking to him when he was in his "wounded martyr" mood, so I threw the weapons and shackles into the back of the Land Rover and climbed into the driver's seat. I didn't start the engine, though. I wasn't about to drive away and leave my father standing alone in the dark. So I made myself comfortable and waited.

Forty minutes later, a set of car headlights appeared on the road and a black Bentley rolled up to my dad. Without a wave or even a look in my direction, he got into the back of the car before the driver even had a chance to get out and open the door for him. The Bentley drove away.

I cranked the engine on the Land Rover and told myself that everything would seem better in the morning. But I knew I was lying to myself. I was about to fly home, leaving Felicity behind, and probably expose myself to an ancient curse that would kill me.

Yeah, things were really looking up.

CHAPTER 17

I ARRIVED IN DEARMONT THE following day, driving up Main Street and past my office. The lights were out and the place looked cold and lonely, despite the bright morning warmth. I felt guilty about leaving without going to visit Felicity again, but she had made it clear that she didn't want to see me, and I'd decided to respect that. That didn't make it hurt any less.

I was tired from a lack of sleep in the hotel last night and a boring flight during which I'd drifted in and out of a light doze. At Bangor International, I'd downed two big cups of coffee before getting into the Land Rover and hitting the road. But even the caffeine couldn't keep me from feeling like death warmed up. I needed my bed in the worst way possible.

When I got to my house, I got out of the Land Rover and glanced over at Felicity's empty house next door. She had loved living there, loved this little town, and loved her job. I still couldn't believe she'd thrown it all away.

I went inside my own house and called out, "Mallory, you here?"

There was no answer other than the low hum of the AC. I cursed my sleep-deprived brain. Of course Mallory wasn't here, her Jeep wasn't on the driveway or street outside. I went upstairs, kicked off my boots, and fell onto the bed, barely able to keep my eyes open. Before I let myself slide into sleep, I checked my phone. No messages. No voice mail. Not a word from Felicity.

I put the phone on the nightstand, not sure what I'd been expecting to see. A text from Felicity saying she'd changed her mind and wanted to come home? That was just wishful thinking. I had to face the fact that I was now the sole employee at Harbinger P.I. That shouldn't be so bad—it was how I'd always run my business before coming to Dearmont—but the thought of arriving at the office to find Felicity's desk empty was depressing.

I closed my eyes, drew in a deep breath, and then let it out slowly, trying to calm my mind. There was no way I was going to sleep if I kept thinking about Felicity. Hell, maybe her staying in England was for the best. If I was going to destroy the sorceress's heart and curse myself to just one more year of life, it wouldn't be fair to grow close to Felicity only to leave her in twelve months' time.

Or would it be better to have a great year and go out with a bang? I was contemplating that question when I smelled something that reminded me of a damp cave. I knew I was in my bedroom and not in an actual cave, but my senses acted as if I were deep underground. The sound of dripping water reached my ears. I'd experienced this sensory overload enough times now to know that it was a memory returning. I kept my eyes closed and waited for my mind to recollect images connected to the memory.

As the images came into focus, I realized I was sitting in a cave that was lit by candles. The candles were positioned around a chalk circle that had been drawn on the stone floor around me. As well as the circle, magical symbols had been drawn on the floor and walls of the cave. In the flickering candlelight, I could make out dark shapes dancing around the circle like liquid shadows, chanting something unintelligible in low, muttered tones.

I watched the dark figures as they danced and I tried to count them. There were nine. Nine women in dark cloaks, their faces hidden in the depths of their cowls.

As the memory played out, I realized that these nine women were the witches of the Coven. There was another figure standing in the shadows, just out of reach of the dim candlelight.

"We will remove it from his mind," one of the witches said softly.

"Lock it away," said another.

"Behind a door."

"A door not to be opened."

"He shall not know what he is."

"All memory of it gone."

"His power is too unpredictable."

"Causing death to those around him."

"Lock it away."

I had no idea what they were talking about. The witches resumed their chanting. I sat still, feeling that I couldn't leave the circle even if I wanted to. My limbs felt heavy. My thoughts were becoming confused.

"Sleep now," one of the witches urged as she danced past my vision.

"When you awaken, all will be well."

"Don't fight it."

"Let the spell carry you away."

"Safe and sound."

"Close your eyes."

"Dream of new things."

"The things we put in your mind."

"Let the dreams become your memories."

My surroundings began to fade into blackness. At first, I thought the candles were being extinguished, but then I understood that it was my mind being snuffed out. The witches' voices became distant. Then, the darkness overtook me.

* * *

"Alec, are you okay?" The female voice woke me up. I sat up on the bed, rubbing my eyes. Had I been dreaming? Then I remembered the childhood memory of sitting in the chalk circle while the Coven cast a spell to lock away part of my mind.

Mallory was leaning over me, her hands on my shoulders, a look of concern on her face. "You were dreaming," she said. "I heard you call out in your sleep."

I felt groggy, disoriented. "Just give me a second. What time is it?"

"It's almost eight."

I'd been asleep for almost ten hours. I slid my legs off the bed and shook my head a couple of times, feeling my awareness of reality returning.

"You look like hell," Mallory said. "I'll put the coffee on." She left the room and I heard her go downstairs.

I sat on the bed for a few minutes longer, until my mind was clear of the thick darkness that I'd either been dreaming about, remembering, or experiencing as I slept. When I felt fully awake, I went down to the kitchen.

Mallory was standing by the sink, pouring steaming coffee into two mugs. She added milk and sugar before handing me one of the mugs and asking, "Are you feeling okay? I got back here hours ago and you've been asleep the whole time. Jet lag that bad, huh?"

"It isn't jet lag," I said, sipping the hot coffee. "I got some of my memories back and it's playing Hell with my mind. I feel like my brain is trying to reboot itself back to a previous operating system installation."

She grinned. "You got your memory back. That's great. So what was the big secret about Paris?"

"The Paris thing isn't really all that much of a revelation. Basically, the *satori* told me to send the box here to myself because there's some prophecy about the Box of Midnight having to be in Dearmont to destroy an ancient evil or something."

Her hazel eyes widened. "Wow, sounds heavy."

"Yeah, but I'm not betting on it being true. Prophecies aren't set in stone. My dad and I were given some information by a coven of witches and it turned out to be wrong."

I told her the details of my trip to London, leaving nothing out except the part about Felicity staying there.

When I was done, I'd almost finished my coffee. I poured us both another and said, "That locked magical door in my mind, the one Devon Blackwell told me about, had nothing to do with Paris. It was put there when I was young. From what I can now remember, the witches that run the Society cast a spell on me."

"What? Why would they do that?"

"I don't know. It happened when I was young, just a kid. There's something they wanted me to forget."

Mallory shrugged. "So what is it?"

"I don't know yet. The memories are returning slowly. They're just fragments that are slowly being pieced together."

"Okay," she said. "We can't do anything about that now. You'll remember in your own time. But from what you just told me, we have a bigger problem. What are we going to do when John DuMont arrives in town looking for that box?"

I shrugged. "I don't know. Apparently, I'm going to destroy the heart inside the box."

"And get cursed? No way, there has to be something else we can do."

I thought about it for a while, drinking my coffee and racking my brain for a solution that didn't involve releasing an ancient curse. "We could move the box," I said. "It wouldn't solve the problem, but it might buy us some time. DuMont knows it's in Dearmont, but he's been too afraid of the prophecy to come for it himself, so he's been sending others to kill me. But now he knows we're onto him, which is why he wasn't at Highgate Cemetery when he was supposed to be. He's probably on his way here now. So we make sure that when he gets here, the box is somewhere else."

Mallory considered what I was saying and nodded her approval. "Okay, it could work. Where are we going to take it?"

"As far away from here as possible. Felicity said the staff only has to be in the vicinity of the box to work and we have no way of knowing how far away the box has to be before the staff can't use its energy."

She drank the last of her coffee and put the mug into the sink. "I have an idea. I'll take the box and you deal with DuMont when he gets here. He needs to be stopped. This could be your best chance. You know he's coming, so you can be ready for him. And as long as I get the box far enough away, he can't use its power. You and that vampire should have a good shot at defeating him."

It was a good plan. Polidori and I might have a chance of killing DuMont if the box was taken out of the equation. I nodded. "Yeah, let's do it."

"I'll leave now," Mallory said, going to the front door and pulling on her boots. "I have a shovel in the Jeep. I'll call you later when I have the box at a safe distance."

I went to her and put a hand on her shoulder. "Be careful, Mallory."

"Don't worry about me. I get the easy job. All I have to do is drive. You have to stay here and fight the bad guy."

"Still, I'm going to worry about you. Wait here." I went down into the basement and picked up an enchanted dagger in a leather sheath. I went back upstairs and gave it to Mallory. "Take this."

"Thanks," she said. "And don't worry, I'll be careful." She kissed me on the cheek and opened the front door. I watched her climb into her orange Jeep and drive away, honking the horn as she pulled away from the curb.

I went back inside and closed the door. Mallory's plan made sense and should give me a chance to defeat DuMont. But an icy tendril of dread slowly slithered up my spine. I couldn't shake the feeling that something really bad was about to happen.

CHAPTER 18

I SPENT THE NEXT HOUR in the basement, preparing for battle. From the array of weapons on the racks, I chose my enchanted sword and an enchanted dagger. I had no idea what magical defenses John DuMont could summon, but enchanted weapons worked against most things, their enchanted blades able to penetrate magical shields.

Along with the dagger and sword, I chose a pistol crossbow like the one I'd used in London and a quiver of bolts. Having a ranged weapon could come in handy.

After attaching the dagger and crossbow to my belt, I carried the sheathed sword upstairs. There was no point putting it on my belt or back just yet because it made driving Hell, and I intended to drive around town looking for DuMont. There was no point waiting for him to come to me.

I just hoped that Mallory had driven far enough away to get the Box of Midnight out of range of DuMont's staff. Without the box's power, the staff was useless, and that was the advantage I was counting on. DuMont would arrive here expecting his staff to get a charge of magical juice from the box. Hopefully, when that didn't happen, he'd be distracted enough with the staff's lack of power that I'd get a chance to strike.

It was a long shot, but it was all I had.

I wondered how many miles Mallory had been able to put between the box and Dearmont, but then remembered that she had to go out to the woods first and dig the damned thing up before she could head out of town. She probably wasn't very far away at all yet.

I fixed myself a chicken sandwich and ate it quickly, washing it down with a Coke before grabbing my keys and heading out of the door. There's nothing like being fueled by chicken and sugar when you need to fight bad guys.

I got into the Land Rover, laying the sheathed sword on the back seat, and wondered where to go first in my search for DuMont. Main Street seemed like a good starting place. I had no idea what Dumont even looked like but was sure I'd know him if I saw him. Practitioners of magic can be recognized by something that is much deeper than mere facial features. It's a feeling like seeing someone you know among a crowd of strangers; your attention is automatically drawn to them. I had no doubt that DuMont would draw my attention the instant I saw him.

I started the engine, then turned it off again when my phone buzzed. It was Mallory.

"What's up?" I asked.

"Alec, we've got a problem. I dug up the box and I drove a couple of miles out of town. But I can't go any farther."

I frowned. "What do you mean?"

"There's some kind of ... force field blocking the road."

I felt suddenly cold. DuMont was here, and he was making sure the box didn't leave the area. "Can you go around it?"

"No, I can see it stretching into the woods on both sides of the road. Then it curves back over Dearmont. It's like a dome."

I got out of the Land Rover and looked up at the evening sky. Sure enough, there was a scintillating purple hue in the night sky. DuMont had put the town on magical lockdown. Everyone was trapped. And DuMont could tap into the power of the box and use the Staff of Midnight.

"Fuck," I whispered into the phone.

"Alec, what are we going to do?"

"I'm going to find DuMont and kill him if I can." I paused, still looking up at the magical barrier surrounding Dearmont. "But if I can't beat him in a fair fight, there's only one other thing I can do. I'll have to destroy the heart inside the box."

"No, that's crazy."

"Mallory, bring the box back here."

"Maybe I can get past this force field somehow. I'll keep trying."

"Just bring the box," I said.

There was a long pause, then Mallory said, "Okay," and hung up.

I put the phone back into my pocket and almost jumped out of my skin when I saw Polidori standing by the Land Rover. He was still sporting his nineteenth century Gothic look and he was smiling.

"I guess you heard that conversation," I said. "DuMont has trapped the entire town in a magical dome. I told Mallory to bring me the box."

"Good," he said. "It's the right thing to do, Alec."

"I'm not going to do anything until I face DuMont in a fight. Destroying the box is only a last resort."

"Of course. As I told you before, I don't trust prophecies any more than you do. So, let's go and find DuMont and attempt to kill him. Perhaps all this nonsense about destroying the box will turn out to be just that: nonsense." He climbed into the Land Rover's passenger seat.

I got in and started the engine. "Don't I have to invite you into my car or something before you get in?"

"Not into your car, no. I can't enter your house unless you invite me in, and I can't see that happening anytime soon."

"You're right about that," I said.

I backed off the driveway and put the Land Rover into gear, but shifted the vehicle back into neutral when I saw Leon Smith's RV approaching. The huge vehicle pulled up alongside us and Leon leaned across his butler, Michael, to speak to me through the open window.

"Hey, Alec, you know anything about the craziness going down on Main Street?"

"What craziness?"

"Heard it on the police scanner. Reports of zombies terrorizing the locals."

"Shit, he's already started raising the dead." I turned to Polidori. "At least we know where to find him."

"Where is the girl with the box?" Polidori asked.

"She's on her way. For someone who doesn't believe in prophecy, it sounds like you can only see this ending one way."

Polidori shrugged. "The destruction of the box is our strongest weapon against DuMont."

"It also carries a death sentence," I reminded him.

"Somebody gonna tell me what's going on?" Leon asked.

"You here to help?" I asked him.

"Yeah, sure."

"We have to kill a necromancer who is raising the dead in downtown Dearmont."

His eyes went wide. "Are you telling me there really are zombies in town?"

I nodded. "And we're going to have to deal with them as well as the necromancer."

"Hell yeah, we're in."

"Good."

Leon pointed at Polidori. "Who's your friend?"

"This is Polidori. He's a vampire."

A worried look crossed Leon's features. "A vampire?" Polidori opened his mouth and extended his fangs, and Leon shrank back from the window slightly. "Okay. We're still in."

"Meet us in the parking lot behind my office building," I said. I put the Land Rover into gear and drove up the street.

"Friends of yours?" Polidori asked, nodding toward the RV behind us.

"Yeah, they're good people."

He turned back to the windshield and sat quietly.

"Can I ask you something?" I said.

"Of course."

"What would happen if you destroyed the box? The curse says that whoever destroys it will have only one year to live, but you're not alive anyway."

He looked amused at my suggestion. "You think I'm going to play around with an ancient Egyptian curse because of the way it's worded? I may not be alive, but you can be sure that if I destroyed the heart of the sorceress in that box, I would meet my end in a year's time."

I shrugged. "It was worth a shot."

He laughed. "You mean it was worth trying to make me take the fall for you."

"No, I was genuinely curious."

"The spirit of the curse will take effect no matter who or what destroys that heart. Arguing over semantics doesn't mean anything when faced with such power."

"Yeah, I guess if anyone knew how to cast curses, it was the ancient Egyptians."

"And Rekhmire was one of the most dangerous," Polidori said. "He almost destroyed the pharaoh's living army with his own, dead one. The curse he cast on that box is powerful indeed."

I sighed and called Mallory. She answered immediately. Her voice sounded worried. "Alec?"

"Meet me in the parking lot behind my office," I said.

"Okay. There's something you should know. The box. It's on my back seat right now and it's doing some weird shit."

"What's happening?"

"There's a purple glow coming from it and the hieroglyphs are moving."

"What do you mean moving?"

"I don't know. Forming different words, maybe. It's freaking me the fuck out."

"Okay, don't worry about it. Just get to the parking lot."

"I will." She hung up.

I wished Felicity were here; she'd know what all this meant.

"The box is opening," Polidori said. "The hieroglyphs line up to form the formula that acts as a key. The process begins when the Staff of Midnight draws on the power of the box. At first, the box only feeds a small amount of power to the staff. Enough, say, to raise a few dead bodies. As the staff continues to draw on the box's power, the box slowly opens. When it is fully open, the staff can use all of the power of the sorceress's heart."

"Great," I said. "So once the box is open, we're screwed."

"Not necessarily. When the box is open, the heart inside is exposed." He looked at me meaningfully.

"Yeah, okay, I get it," I said. "When the box opens, I destroy the heart. Message received, loud and clear."

Maybe some prophecies couldn't be avoided after all.

CHAPTER 19

As SOON AS WE HIT Main Street, the extent of the problem became apparent. Townsfolk ran in panic or hid behind parked vehicles while at least a dozen animated corpses roamed the street. The zombies were little more than skeletons dressed in the clothes they'd been buried in, including Union Army frock coats. Some of the undead wore tattered Victorian gowns. The horde of walking corpses lurched back and forth along Main Street, spreading panic by gnashing their teeth and reaching for the residents of Dearmont with skeletal hands.

"This is just the beginning," Polidori said. "As the staff grows in power, DuMont will raise more and more of these mindless abominations."

I wasn't sure where he got off calling the zombies abominations, since he landed squarely in that category himself, as far as I was concerned. I parked in my usual space behind the office and got out, bringing the sword from the back seat with me and attaching the sheath to my belt.

Michael parked the RV next to the Land Rover and jumped down to the ground, a shotgun in his hands. Leon came around the vehicle, similarly armed, and said, "You see those things?"

"Yeah, I saw them," I said. "Let's send them back to where they came from." I unsheathed the sword and it glowed brightly in my hand.

I led Polidori, Leon, and Michael along the side of the building and onto Main Street. The scene was total mayhem. A man in his sixties ran past us, screaming. His pursuer, a skeleton dressed in a frock coat and string tie, approached us and clattered its teeth together.

I swung the sword at its neck, severing the spinal column and sending the skull tumbling to the sidewalk. When it landed, Leon crushed it beneath his boot, the old bone breaking easily. The body dropped to the ground as if it were a marionette whose strings had been cut.

"Aim for their heads," I said. "Just like in the movies and on TV." I stepped into the road where zombie in a voluminous golden gown was shambling toward a petrified mother holding her baby and shrinking back against the window of a clothing store. An abandoned stroller stood on the sidewalk a few feet away. The poor woman had probably just been taking her baby on a pleasant evening walk when she'd been confronted with the chaos that Main Street had become.

I sliced the head off the zombie and shouted to the woman, "You need to get home and lock all your doors and windows. Now."

She nodded, clutching the baby tightly. "I will. Thank you."

I turned back to the main group of undead. Shotgun blasts rang in the air as Michael and Leon opened fire. A couple of the zombies fell but still more continued to shamble toward the people fleeing along the street. Polidori moved with blinding speed and ripped off the heads of a half dozen of the walking dead.

Along with the sound of shotgun blasts, screams, and shouts, another sound filled the air: the strident wail of police sirens. Two police cruisers arrived, skidding to a stop outside Dearmont Donuts. Sheriff Cantrell got out of the lead car, his daughter Amy out of the other. They had their guns drawn and the sheriff shouted something I couldn't quite hear at the shambling horde of zombies.

What the hell was he doing? Trying to arrest them?

I sprinted along the sidewalk toward him. "That's not going to work," I said. "They won't come peacefully."

Amy seemed to have realized that fact and fired her handgun at a zombie Union soldier who had been lurching toward her car until her shot penetrated its skull and it dropped like a sack of moldy potatoes.

Sheriff Cantrell turned to me with anger burning in his eyes. "You! I should have realized this would be connected to you, Harbinger. Drop that weapon and turn around. You're under arrest."

"If you arrest me, this problem is only going to get worse," I said. "I'm the only one who can stop this craziness."

Speaking of stopping the craziness, where the hell was Mallory with the box? I hoped she hadn't run into any zombies on her way back here from the edge of town.

"I said drop the sword and turn around," Cantrell said, reaching for his cuffs.

"Dad," Amy said, "shouldn't we let Alec sort this mess out? God knows it's beyond our pay grade."

"You stay out of this, Amy. You know what these people are like with their preternatural bullshit. Your mother would be alive today if it wasn't for one of these investigators." He spat out the final word distastefully.

When he mentioned Amy's mother, I looked toward the zombies, expecting to see Mary Cantrell lumbering around among the other animated dead. But the zombies were all dressed in much older fashions than the red dress Mary Cantrell had been buried in.

I knew where DuMont was.

"Dad," Amy said, letting off another shot and dropping another zombie, "we don't have time for this." She pointed down Main Street where a second horde of zombies was approaching.

The sheriff looked at me with disdain, but then said, "Fine. I'll deal with you later." He moved his considerable bulk to the middle of the street and began firing into the mass of dead bodies walking toward us.

I looked at Amy. "Thanks."

"Don't mention it. But you have to stop this, Alec. If you know what to do, please do it now."

"I know what do," I said.

I went over to where Polidori was standing a few feet away. He'd obviously been listening to my conversation with Amy.

"Yes, you know what to do," he said.

I called Mallory. As soon as she answered the call, I said, "Meet me at the South Cemetery."

"Okay." I could hear the engine of her Jeep in the background, revving hard as she sped back to town.

"And be careful. There are zombies everywhere and probably a lot more at the cemetery." I ended the call and said to Polidori, "Come on. I know where DuMont is. The cemetery manager told me that the South Cemetery is full of graves and has been for a hundred years. Judging by the clothing on these things, that's where they came from. That's where we'll find DuMont."

Leon was standing next to Michael and happily blasting away at the zombies coming up the road. I clapped him on the shoulder. "I'm going to try and cut this off at the source. You okay here?"

"Yeah, man, no problem at all. We'll see you later."

Polidori and I ran over to the Land Rover and got in. I gunned the engine and backed out of the parking space before racing toward Main Street. To get to the South Cemetery, I was going to have to go through the horde of zombies on the road, and I intended to do just that: go through them.

I turned south on Main Street and accelerated toward the mass of skeletons ahead. Polidori braced himself for impact and I did the same, gripping the wheel tightly as we plowed into the animated dead.

Bones cracked and splintered against the hood and crunched beneath the tires as the Land Rover cut a swath through the shambling horde. When we made it through to the other side and were clear of the zombies, Polidori looked through the back window and nodded. "Quite impressive."

Shots rang out as Leon, Michael, the sheriff, and Amy began firing at the walking skeletons that had survived the Land Rover onslaught.

I drove toward the South Cemetery, ready to gun the engine again if we met another wave of the risen dead. We didn't. When we got to the cemetery, I crashed through the iron gates and into the graveyard.

Dennis Jackson, the cemetery manager, needed to get his crew down here to maintain the grounds better, because the South Cemetery was overgrown with weeds and long grass, as well as ivy that clung to the mausoleums and gravestones. The trees were also untended and overgrown, making it seem like nature was attempting to reclaim this resting place of the long-forgotten dead.

"Look there," Polidori said, pointing through the windshield at a purple glow emanating beyond the trees.

We got out of the Land Rover and I started for the trees.

"Wait, what are you doing?" Polidori asked. "We should wait for your friend and the Box of Midnight. That's the only way we're going to stop DuMont."

"I came here to face him," I said, marching toward the trees with my sword in hand. Polidori might think that I should just destroy the box immediately, but I wanted to explore other options, for obvious reasons. If I could stop DuMont without having to resort to cursing myself, all the better. At least it would buy me some time, during which I could maybe find a way to defeat Rekhmire.

Polidori followed me into the trees. The cemetery was dark, lit only by the purple glow ahead and the blue energy emanating from my sword.

We emerged from the trees into a large open area where gravestones and tombs jutted up from the long grass like uneven teeth. Every grave looked as if it had burst open and standing next to each tombstone was a zombie. They were dressed in the fashions of a hundred years ago or more, each one standing still as if awaiting orders. The air smelled of freshly-turned dirt and moldy cloth.

The man who was surely going to give those orders stood on top of a gray stone mausoleum, the Staff of Midnight held aloft in his hand, the purple glow pulsing from it in waves of power that spread over the cemetery.

DuMont was dressed in a dark suit and tie, as if he had just stepped out of a board meeting. His black hair waved wildly as if it were caught by a strong wind even though the night was calm.

He looked at me and a sneer crossed his lips. "Harbinger, I knew you would come. It has been prophesied that we are to meet here tonight."

"Then you also know what else has been prophesied," I said. "If I destroy the heart of the sorceress, that staff of yours dies, along with this army of zombies." I indicated the undead who stood by their graves, eerily silent but also seeming to be watching us.

"Not every prophecy comes true," he said. "For too long, I have been afraid of facing you because of the utterings of a few witches. But I serve a power that is far greater than you and all those witches combined. I have nothing to fear. Kill him, my children." He swept the staff around himself and then pointed its tip at me.

The zombies lurched into action, stepping forward, arms outstretched as they reached for me.

I sighed. "I've already killed a load of these guys in town, DuMont. Are you going to make me kill more of them?" From what I'd see so far, the animated skeletons were pretty easy to destroy.

He grinned. "Those were weak, raised when the staff was barely beginning to gather its power. With each second, the power grows. These undead are much stronger than the ones I raised earlier."

I took a swing at the zombie closest to me, a skeleton dressed in a tattered black suit. As my blade was about to reach the neck and sever it, the zombie dodged the attack. It grabbed my throat in a tight, bony grip and began to choke the life out of me.

I looked over at Polidori. He was having troubles of his own, trying to fend off a half dozen zombies that had rushed him. These undead were definitely faster than the ones in town.

I lashed out with my boot and connected with the ribs of the skeleton who was trying to strangle me. Its grip loosened slightly and I thrust the sword up into its shoulder, cutting off the arm that had me in its grip. The skeleton tried again with the other arm but I didn't underestimate it this time. I chopped off its head with a swift blow. The body fell to the ground with a rattle of bones.

I positioned my body in a defensive stance, waiting to see which of the advancing zombies was going to attack next. The problem was, there were hundreds of the damned things, and still more crawling out of graves and busting their way out of the mausoleums.

Polidori had dispatched his attackers and backed up to where I was standing. "There are too many of them," he said. "We won't win this."

Dumont laughed. "You might as well lie down and die now, Harbinger. This graveyard is only the beginning. Can you feel the power growing? It calls to them. It calls them from the grave. Soon the dead shall rise across all the Earth."

I could feel the staff's power intensifying. The purple glow now lit the entire cemetery and there was a crackling energy in the air that I hadn't noticed before, and it was growing in strength by the second. If I had the Box of Midnight here right now, I would destroy it without a second thought. The kind of energy that was flying around the cemetery was too dangerous to let anyone wield, much less a man like DuMont, who wanted to help his master bring about an apocalypse.

Beyond the trees, I heard the screech of tires and a car door slamming. A few seconds later, Mallory appeared, holding the Box of Midnight at arms' length. The box had changed. It had opened like a flower and at its center I could see a pulsing heart, the heart of the ancient sorceress, Tia. Each beat of the heart emitted a wave of purple energy that spread into the air to intensify the energy already there. It fed the power that DuMont controlled.

DuMont himself had become imbued with the power of the sorceress's heart. His eyes glowed the same purple as the air around him and sparks of power ran from the Staff of Midnight along his arm and into his chest.

I needed to get to the box, to destroy its power, but there were fifty or sixty undead in my way. I cried out and lunged forward, hacking and slashing at them in an attempt to reach the box before DuMont absorbed so much power that he was unbeatable. Polidori joined me, lashing at the zombies with his clawed hands, pulling them to pieces.

But for every monster we killed, another two took its place until the skeletons stood between us and the box like an impenetrable wall of bone and malevolence.

I saw Mallory place the box on the ground. She reached down to her belt and unsheathed the enchanted dagger I'd given her earlier. Kneeling next to the box, she looked down at the beating sorceress's heart and raised the dagger above her head, its blue glow highlighting the grim determination on her face.

"Mallory, no!" I shouted. I began attacking the zombies wildly, desperate to reach Mallory before she brought the dagger down.

But even as my cry was still ringing in the air, Mallory plunged the dagger into the heart of the sorceress.

The heart exploded in a blast of scarlet light that made it appear for a moment that Mallory were covered in blood. But the light faded as it was absorbed into Mallory's body. She looked at me with frightened eyes before falling heavily to the ground.

"No!" I cried out. I felt hot, stinging tears spill from my eyes as I lashed out at the monsters around me. Pieces of shattered bone flew everywhere as I hacked a path toward Mallory. The zombies were weaker now, the purple glow in the air dissipating.

I got to the trees, leaving Polidori to deal with the undead. The Box of Midnight had been blackened by the energy of the scarlet explosion. The heart at its center was black and dead and unmoving, its pulse gone.

"Mallory," I said, reaching down to check her neck for a pulse. I found one, but it was weak and uneven, like the flutter of a butterfly's wings.

I stood and turned to face DuMont. He was still standing atop the mausoleum, the staff in his hand dead, but with the power in his body still glowing out through his eyes. His face was contorted into a grimace of anger.

The zombies had all fallen to the ground, the power that had once animated them gone.

"She ruined it," DuMont snarled. "She ruined the Box of Midnight. Never mind a year to live; I'm going to kill her myself, now." He floated down to the ground and stalked toward us.

Polidori rushed to stop him but DuMont waved his hand and the vampire was thrown across the cemetery. I didn't see where he landed; I couldn't focus on anything except DuMont and cold ball of rage building within me.

I would not let him kill Mallory.

The cold ball of rage felt like something tangible in my body, rising from my chest and shooting along my arms to my hands. I dropped the sword to the ground. Its blue light extinguished as soon I released the hilt but there was another glow now, a deep blue light emanating from my hands. It formed itself into simple shapes that then resolved themselves into complex magical circles.

DuMont stopped in his tracks. His eyes, which still glowed purple, went wide with surprise. "No, it can't be."

I looked at him, feeling my anger compress itself into the glowing magical circles that had formed around my hands. The energy was building itself up to a critical mass. "Don't ever think you can hurt my friends," I whispered to him.

I drew my arms back slightly, then thrust them forward, releasing the magical energy from my hands. It shot forward and hit DuMont, exploding into a shower of bright blue sparks. He was thrown back against a mausoleum. I heard bones break as his body was slammed into the stone. He slid to the ground and lay, unmoving. Blood trickled from his mouth and ears. There was no doubt that he was dead.

I looked down at my hands, which had returned to normal, and wondered what the hell had just happened.

CHAPTER 20

BY THE TIME I GOT home, a light rain had begun to fall. I'd left my Land Rover at the cemetery and driven back in Mallory's Jeep, with her lying on the back seat. When I got to my house, I picked her up and carried her inside, laying her gently on the sofa and going into the kitchen to make coffee. She was shivering slightly, so a hot drink would help warm her up.

Outside, the rain began to pour down, hitting the kitchen window hard and sliding down the glass in wet smears. When the coffee was done, I took it into the living room and set it on the table by the sofa. Mallory stirred and opened her eyes.

"Hey," I said.

She smiled. "Hey." Sitting up, she looked around the room. "How did I get back here?"

"I brought you home. What's the last thing you remember?"

"Stabbing that damn heart. After that, nothing, until I woke up just now."

"How do you feel?" I asked, passing her the coffee.

She took a moment to consider that. "I feel ... different. Like there's something inside me that wasn't there before. I don't know, I can't explain it."

"When you stabbed the sorceress's heart, you absorbed ... something. It was a red glow that came out of the heart and went into your body."

"Yeah, it's called a curse."

I looked at her seriously. "I wish you hadn't done it, Mallory."

"Yeah, but if I hadn't, we'd be living in a world full of zombies right now."

"True, but it wasn't your responsibility."

She looked at me incredulously. "But it was yours?"

"It comes with the job."

She shrugged. "Well, it's too late to argue about that now. What's done is done."

"And cannot be undone," I said flatly.

"Don't say that, Alec. I'm relying on you to get me out of this mess."

"You really think I can do that?"

She smiled but her eyes looked sad. "Yeah, I do. It's your responsibility. It comes with the job, remember?"

"Mallory, I don't think I can do that. The curse is...."

She put a finger against my lips. "Don't say it. I know the curse is ancient and powerful, but even as I sank the dagger into that heart, I trusted that you would find a way for me to beat this. If anyone in the world can, it's you."

"I'll try," I said. "I'll do everything I can."

"I know you will." She stroked my cheek and stood up. "But, just in case I do only have twelve months to live, I have to go."

"What? Go where?"

"I have to find Mister Scary. That's more important to me now more than ever. I only have a year to find him."

"But you don't have to go right now." I went to her and put my hands on her shoulders. "Stay tonight at least. Maybe in the morning…."

"In the morning, I'll be somewhere else, Alec. I can't stay here."

"But you don't have any leads."

"Something will turn up."

"I can't believe you're leaving. I thought you were going to stay around for a while."

"So did I. But things between us were getting too intimate, Alec. It was going to swing one way or the other and I was happy enough to stick around and see which way it played out. But I can't do that now. What if we decide we want to be together? I only have a year left. I can't ask you to love me, knowing that I'll be leaving you so soon."

"We can make it work," I said.

She shook her head. "No, I have to find Mister Scary. I'm sorry, Alec, but I have to go. I'll get my things."

She went upstairs and I heard her gathering her things from the bedroom and bathroom. When she came down, she had a sports bag slung over one shoulder. In her hand was the enchanted dagger I'd given her, the one she'd plunged into the heart of the sorceress. "I guess I should give you this back." She held out the glowing dagger.

"No, you keep it. You might need it," I said.

"Okay, thanks." She sheathed the dagger and said, "I'll give it back to you someday."

I didn't like the tone of finality in her voice. "You know you can call me anytime," I said.

"I know, and maybe I will. Maybe I'll need help kicking some paranormal butt. Anyway, you call me when you find a cure for this curse, okay?"

"Yeah," I said, "I'll do that." We both knew this was nothing more than bravado. Ancient Egyptian curses cast by powerful sorcerers weren't exactly reversible. But we went through the motions anyway. It was going to make this goodbye much easier.

She went to the front door and opened it. "Wow, looks like a storm." The rain hissed down over the street, the Land Rover, and Mallory's Jeep. She turned to me and kissed me briefly on the lips. "Goodbye, Alec." She turned and ran through the downpour to her orange Jeep and got in quickly, starting the engine as soon as she was inside. Her headlights illuminated the falling raindrops.

I walked out onto the driveway, ignoring the cold rain that pelted down on me. It soaked through my clothing and chilled my skin as I walked to the end of the driveway and then onto the sidewalk in front of the house, watching the tail lights of Mallory's Jeep as it disappeared down the street. She made a left turn toward town, and then she was gone.

Turning back toward my driveway, I felt a sudden weakness in my body, as if I'd been drained of all my energy. I'd only felt this weak once before in my life, when I was bed-bound with glandular fever as a child. But even then, the feeling of weakness hadn't come on so suddenly.

I reached out for the Land Rover to support myself but I missed it and stumbled away onto the front lawn. My legs gave way and I collapsed to the cold, wet grass. I couldn't move. Even breathing seemed like an effort. I lay looking at the square of light beyond my open front door, knowing that although it was only a few feet away, it might as well be a thousand miles.

Whatever it was that I'd done to DuMont earlier in the cemetery, I was now paying the price for it.

All I could do was lie here and wait to regain my strength.

The smell of the rain on the grass brought back a memory, a memory that had been locked behind the magical door but was now clicking into place in the fragmented part of my mind. I remembered that when I was young, maybe nine-years-old, I'd been attacked by

Tommy Lyle, a bully at my school in Oregon. Tommy had been much older than me and for some reason had taken a strong dislike to me. While I was walking home from school one rainy afternoon, Tommy and a group of his friends had come out of the Seven Eleven and seen me walking next to the railroad tracks that led in the direction of home.

The group of boys, and two girls, had intercepted me by the tracks and Tommy had started pushing me around. Even at the age of nine, I'd instinctively known that if I gave in to Tommy now, and let him beat me without a fight, I'd never be free of him. He would always see me as an easy target. So, I'd fought back. Tommy and I had exchanged punches in the rain by the tracks and at one point, the much-larger boy had knocked me down. I'd landed face down in the wet grass and the anger I'd felt at these bullies grew into a ball of fury that couldn't control.

I remembered getting back up, tears of rage burning my eyes. I remembered Tommy and his friends laughing at me. I remembered bright blue energy that crackled from my hands. Timmy's eyes went wide when I hurled the energy at him. The force of the blast threw him across the railroad tracks, where his friends ran over to him and helped him to his feet before running away. Tommy was dazed and his friends looked frightened. As they fled, they shouted back words like, "Freak!" and "Weirdo!"

Then my memory moved forward to the cave and the witches and the chalk circle, the time when the magical door was being put in my mind. And I knew who the figure in the shadows, the figure watching the proceedings, was. Just before I fell into the enchanted sleep the witches put on me, I looked across the cave and for a moment, the flickering light reached the features of the man standing in the shadows. It was my father.

The memory played itself out as I lay on the lawn and then receded as I returned to the present. I felt so cold and magically drained that if I didn't get inside soon, I was going to perish out here. Wouldn't that be ironic? Alec Harbinger, preternatural investigator, dies on his own front lawn in the rain.

I heard a car coming up the street. Maybe it was one of the neighbors, or maybe even Mallory returning. Whoever it was, I had to do something to attract their attention. But I still couldn't move and the car stopped before it reached me. I heard the engine idling. Then a car door opened and closed and the vehicle turned around and headed back the way it had come.

I could hear high heels picking rapidly on the driveway next door, then a worried voice. "Alec?" The heels came across the lawn toward me and then I felt a pair of warm arms around my neck.

I managed to turn my head and look up to see a familiar face. Her dark eyes were hidden by the rain on her glasses, but even in my current state, I recognized her instantly.

"Felicity."

She tried to help me to my feet but I was still too weak to move.

"Felicity," I said again. My mouth seemed to be the only part of me that was working.

"At least you know who I am," she said, an edge of concern in her voice.

I managed to get to my knees with her help. We stumbled together across the wet grass toward the open front door and the light and warmth beyond.

Of course I knew who Felicity was.

But with all the memories flooding back to me, memories of some kind of magical power that had been inside me all of my life, I wasn't sure I knew who I was anymore.

THE END

LOST SOUL

BURIED MEMORY

DARK MAGIC

DEAD GROUND

To join the Harbinger P.I. mailing list and get news of new releases in the series:

http://eepurl.com/bRehez

36814914R00224

Made in the USA
San Bernardino, CA
27 May 2019

Made in the USA
San Bernardino, CA
16 September 2017